Sun Up in Sin Town...

Without the neons lighting the joints and the jukeboxes blaring and the fly-cats and kittens and winos and squares frolicking up and down the wide walks, Third Street was just another dismal-looking slum street. To a guy not in the know it would seem that all the sin peddlers and buyers had crawled into their respective cribs for the morning. But Tabor knew better. Nothing had been changed but the locations. In the smoky dim-lit back rooms and basements the cats and kittens and squares were still playing, the kittens selling it to the squares and putting it on the cats just for kicks.

William H. Duhart Bibliography
(1921-2003)

Novels:
The Deadly Pay-Off (Gold Medal, 1958)
Ravishing Seductress (Merit, 1963)

Stories (alphabetical listing):
Darling of Hate! (*Off Beat Detective Stories*, January 1962)
The Devil's Caress (*Shock Mystery Tales Magazine*, March 1962)
Die in My Embrace, Darling! (*Keyhole Detective Story Magazine*, January 1962)
Fear Stacks the Deck (*Web Detective Stories*, September 1961)
Lust of the Damned! (*Off Beat Detective Stories*, September 1961)
Lust Won't Wait! (*Off Beat Detective Stories*, May 1962)
Never Con a Killer! (*Off Beat Detective Stories*, July 1961)
Never Fool with Passion! (*Off Beat Detective Stories*, July 1962)
Passion Swamp! (*Keyhole Detective Story Magazine*, September 1962)
Some Dames Are Poison! (*Off Beat Detective Stories*, September 1962)
Too Lovely to Live! (*Keyhole Detective Story Magazine*, June 1962)

Film Scripts (all unproduced):
Cut, Shuffle and Deal (1959)
The Big Mistake (1959)
Rock Candy Laughter (1959)
The Truth Pill (1959)
No Love, No Mercy (1959)
Lullaby of Vengeance (1959)

The Deadly Pay-Off
William H. Duhart

Introduction by Bill Kelly

Black Gat Books • Eureka California

THE DEADLY PAY-OFF

Published by Black Gat Books
A division of Stark House Press
1315 H Street
Eureka, CA 95501, USA
griffinskye3@sbcglobal.net
www.starkhousepress.com

THE DEADLY PAY-OFF
Published by Gold Medal Books, Greenwich,
and copyright © 1958 by Fawcett Publications, Inc.

All rights reserved under International
and Pan-American Copyright Conventions.

"The Deadly Pay-Off: An Introduction"
copyright © 2022 by Bill Kelly

ISBN: 979-8-88601-010-7

Cover design by Jeff Vorzimmer, ¡caliente!design, Austin, Texas
Text design by Mark Shepard, shepgraphics.com
Proofreading by Bill Kelly
Cover art by Al Brulé

PUBLISHER'S NOTE:
This is a work of fiction. Names, characters, places and
incidents are either the products of the author's imagination or
used fictionally, and any persons to actual persons, living
or dead, events or locales, is entirely coincidental.
Without limiting the rights under copyright reserved above, no
part of this publication may be reproduced, stored, or
introduced into a retrieval system or transmitted in any form
or by any means (electronic, mechanical, photocopying,
recording or otherwise) without the prior written permission of
both the copyright owner and the above publisher of the book.

First Stark House Press/Black Gat Edition: December 2022

The Deadly Pay-Off:
An Introduction

By Bill Kelly

William Hector Duhart was born on January 30, 1921 and died on January 14, 2003. His brief career as a published author was bookended by two novels, *The Deadly Pay-Off* (Gold Medal 805, 1958) and *Ravishing Seductress* (Merit Books 667, 1963), both paperback originals. French publisher Gallimard reprinted *The Deadly Pay-Off* as *Nib d'amour!* in 1960 as part of its Série noire imprint, translation by Frank Degrémont. Sandwiched between the two novels were eleven short stories, published in the years 1961 and 1962, most of which appeared the pulp magazines *Off Beat Detective* and *Keyhole Detective Story Magazine*, both of these ventures being relatively short-lived and coming as the pulp magazine era was drawing to a close. Both magazines featured author lineups that included notable practitioners of the mystery short story form, so Duhart found himself in good company, but he was not to have any magazine credits after 1962.

Information relating to Duhart's life is scarce, but after being paroled from Waupun State Prison (Wisconsin) in 1957 for assault and armed robbery, his literary career was off to a promising start as he was one of two African-American in residence (the other being Charles Wright [*The Messenger*]) at the prestigious Handy Writers' Colony in Marshall, Illinois from 1957 to 1958. Duhart worked with Lowney Turner Handy, mentor of novelist James Jones (*From Here to Eternity* / *Some Came Running*) and with

Jones himself, who in a *Sepia* December, 1957 magazine article regarded Duhart as "a man to be reckoned with."

Duhart had hopes of seeing *The Deadly Pay-Off* made into a motion picture. Among his letters preserved by The University of Illinois at Springfield is a letter to MCA Studio executive Ned Brown regarding this possibility. What is intriguing about the Brown letter and the others in this collection is that they are all dated 1956, which indicates that *The Deadly Pay-Off* was written, at least in draft form, prior to Duhart being released from prison in 1957. In any case a movie was not made, but of course the novel was published by Gold Medal (#805) in 1958. Apparently, Duhart did not stop knocking on the Hollywood door, because the Library of Congress Catalog of Copyright Entries for 1960 lists several Duhart 1959 screenplay copyrights. Titles include *Rock Candy Laughter*, *Lullaby of Vengeance*, *The Truth Pill*, *No Love, No Mercy* and *Cut, Shuffle and Deal*.

With the publishing of *Ravishing Seductress* in 1963, Duhart's career as a published author came to end. He died at the age of 81 and was buried in Abraham Lincoln National Cemetery in Elwood, Illinois, his right as a WW II US Army veteran. His tombstone reads "Gone But Not Forgotten".

The Deadly Pay-Off's protagonist, Tank Tabor, is professional gambler in 1950's Milwaukee. Tabor is not directly linked to the organized crime syndicate run by Arky Calahan, whose power is absolute and whose corruptive influence extends not only throughout the criminal element, but into law enforcement as well. Tabor continuously walks a high wire in an effort not to run afoul of Calahan's interests and has succeeded in doing so for years. Tabor's life becomes further complicated when Tank's brother Bill, a private investigator, is hired by Tabor's ex-flame Tess Andrews to look into the murder of her husband, a witness to the murder of a journalist who came too close to Calahan's operations:

> This was the game, he [Tank] thought. Somebody was always trying to uncover somebody else's trash. Now it was his kid brother Bill digging in Calahan's backyard. The kid sure as hell didn't know how to pick his people. He had climbed up on a guy's back who, with just a nod, could have him turned into cemetery feed in no time flat.

Calahan summons Tabor and orders him to persuade his brother Bill to drop the investigation, knowing that Tabor's livelihood, if not his life, depends upon Calahan's continued good will. Tank agrees to intercede, but both Bill and Tess refuse to cooperate. Tank's relationships with both Bill and Tess are complicated by past pain and guilt and he is further troubled by the fact that both accuse him of being nothing more than a weakling stooge for Calahan. Tank attempts to buy some time in the hope of bringing Bill and Tess around, but Calahan's fear of exposure drives him to action:

> "You know the way the game goes, Tank. What you can't control, you crush."

Doing the crushing are Calahan's "associates", Trigger Slim, Croaker and Monkey Face Moe. The colorful "monikers" Duhart uses to name Calahan's goons are stylistically in concert with the language used throughout, both for dialogue and exposition. Duhart was attempting to create a criminal milieu tapestry that accurately reflected both the people and the world they moved in. As a former criminal himself,

Duhart of course brings some credibility to his efforts, but I suspect that he was also enthralled with the use of language itself, seeking to craft his prose and not merely "salt" the story with realistic-sounding verbiage:

> Tabor wanted to give up some more lip, but the click of the hammer going back on Moe's .45 sounded like the hike of a ratchet jack. The gun's bore peeping at him over the window ledge of the Buick looked a foot round.
>
> Whatever kind of game Nina-gal was playing, evidently she was playing it like a champ. It would seem that the lovely was squeezing every dram of the gravy from the golden goose.

This Stark House Press edition of *The Deadly Pay-Off* features a "Glossary of Underworld Lingo" that should help the reader with definitions that might not be entirely clear from the context in which they are used.

Calahan's men proceed to do their worst and Tabor finds himself framed for drug dealing and corrupting a minor as Calahan devises a scheme, with the help of corrupt police and politicians, that will send Tank to prison for twenty years. After being arrested Tank meets Jock Adams, a black inmate who has previously worked for Calahan, but has now fallen out of favor with the crime boss. The men form an unlikely alliance, Tabor, who trusts no one, and Jock who is eager to even the score with Calahan. Duhart ensures that their alliance is believable by deft characterization wherein each man's actions are true to their nature. Jock and Tank both seek to understand the why of their alliance; Jock opens with:

> "You'd trust me with your ten grand? You
> don't even know me."

"I don't have much of a choice. It's either I trust you to come through or sit here like a nut and wait for Arky Calahan to murder my brother and lose me in the penitentiary. I'll place my bets on you."

And Jock again:

> "This is something new. Somebody trusting
> me. You know something, man?"
> "What's that?"

"I kinda like the feeling of being trusted. Even though it's a forced issue." He stuck out his ham-sized hand and Tabor gripped it. The big guy didn't have a hand, he had a vice. They finished trying to crush each other's bones to a fine powder and Jock said: "You picked yourself a winner, man. I don't understand it, but I'll be damned if you didn't."

Each man is aware that he is clearly taking a risk, and although the implied trust is somewhat tentative, both are clearly the better off for this new partnership. Jock and Tank continue to work together throughout, with some peaks and valleys in the relationship.

Jock is also a friend of Tess, so his interest in the outcome is not limited to getting even with Calahan or his avowed alliance with Tank. After a bump in their relationship that leaves Tank feeling guilty for not having trusted him, Jock reaffirms his commitment by explaining:

> "Maybe it's the way you made me feel when
> you trusted me with your geets [money].
> Nobody ever took me at face value before.
> Then maybe it's because Tess thinks you're
> worth helping."

Despite Calahan's best efforts to manipulate the justice system, Tank gets bailed out of jail, but almost immediately finds his hole dug deeper as he becomes the victim of another frame, this time for murder. As pushed as far as he can go by Calahan's puppet mastering and the heinous acts committed by his underlings, Tank is faced with a dilemma: he wants revenge, but murdering Calahan and / or his men will put him on the run for life, so he attempts to determine Calahan's role in two earlier murders, thereby putting Calahan on the hook and taking himself off. Duhart's construction of the story narrative employs an accelerated pacing technique: as the danger increases, so does the pace of the action. Even at the outset of the book, events furthering the story move along briskly: expository passages are woven concisely as bite-size pieces within the current action. Dialogue and exposition are also interwoven so that there are no protracted examples of either, stylistic choices that can be deadly to an action / suspense narrative. As the novel approaches mid-point, Tank realizes that, short of killing him, there is little Calahan can do to further harm him. He goes for broke and the narrative becomes a page turner. He begins to track down all the underworld characters that might have knowledge of the murders of Tess's husband and the journalist and begins to sort out their stories, and for those with a grudge against Calahan, their cooperation. He enters a world he is familiar with but, courtesy of Calahan, a world that is now determinedly set against him:

> Without the neons lighting the joints and the jukeboxes blaring and the fly-cats and kittens and winos and squares frolicking up and down the wide walks, Third Street was just another dismal-looking slum street. To a

> guy not in the know it would seem that all the
> sin peddlers and buyers had crawled into
> their respective cribs for the morning. But
> Tabor knew better. Nothing had been changed
> but the locations. In the smoky dim-lit back
> rooms and basements the cats and kittens
> and squares were still playing, the kittens
> selling it to the squares and putting it on the
> cats just for kicks.

Throughout the novel it is clear that Duhart is working against a common literary cliché, a cliché then and now: Tank is never a hero-figure wrecking violent revenge on those who have wronged him. As the story proceeds, we see that Tank relies more on his brain than he does on violence. Repeatedly we see him resist the temptation to go gunning for Calahan and his men. Tank progressively adds to his team of those united against Calahan, all fearful but able to muster the courage to work toward Calahan's downfall. His allies include Nina, a prostitute living as she does because she has no other options. Tank offers her a way out and she has the courage and determination to take it, knowing the possible consequences:

> Nina stood suddenly and gave him what she
> thought was a smile. He gave her E for effort
> but the smile was about as strong as a piece of
> overcooked spaghetti. It slithered all over her
> face.

In the end Tank devises a plan that brings matters to a head, but for each step of the way he is accompanied by those with as much courage and grit as he himself possesses.

William H. Duhart may have made a limited

appearance on the crime fiction scene, but it is one that reveals a great deal of skill, a love of language and perhaps, great potential, had he been able to publish more. *The Deadly Pay-Off* is a first novel and this evidences itself in his portrayal of Calahan and his three henchmen. Duhart was so familiar with these characters and their world that he seems to take little interest in their characterizations—in a literary sense, he takes them for granted—they are "bad guys" pure and simple. His "good guy" characterizations are more well-developed and detailed; the criminals and crooked cops have a prop-like quality, and with one or two exceptions, they emerge as cutouts. One of Duhart's creative virtues, his love of language, is at times perhaps overdone: for instance, a term like "gunsel" is repeated several times within a limited number of lines. Relatively speaking, some shallow minor character development and redundant use of vocabulary emerge as quibbles compared to the plotting, characterizations of the major figures and the sheer vitality of the prose that engage the reader throughout to produce a page turner, but not a shallow "action hero" potboiler.

African-Americans, whether as authors or fictional protagonists were a mystery genre rarity as Duhart was in prison composing *The Deadly Pay-Off*. As the 1950s drew to a close, black authors Chester Himes and John B. West were just emerging. Himes of course, wrote several novels featuring the black detectives Grave Digger Jones and Coffin Ed Johnson. Conversely, West's protagonist was Rocky Steele, a white private investigator. Ed Lacy, a white author, featured black protagonists in some of his stories and novels. Prior to the aforementioned authors, published mystery fiction by black authors was indeed a rarity: Rudolph Fisher produced *The Conjure-Man Dies* in

1932, featuring black detective Dr. John Archer, who was to appear in only one additional short-fiction work in 1935, "John Archer's Nose". George S. Schuyler (writing as William Stockton) wrote many mystery and spy fiction stories, most of them appearing as serials in the *Pittsburg Courier*, an African-American weekly newspaper. But it would seem that Duhart might have been beginning his career just as opportunities were beginning to open up for black crime fiction writers. He had to be encouraged by having *The Deadly Pay-Off* selected as a Gallimard Série noire publication. However, based upon the number of film scripts he copyrighted, Duhart may have had his sights set on bigger rewards than paperback original houses like Gold Medal could provide. However, in any case, Duhart's disappears from the world of published fiction, with his final known work, 1963's *Ravishing Seductress*.

Although a first novel, *The Deadly Pay-Off*, with Duhart appearing to find his way at times, possesses a protagonist more clever than brutal, some well-defined characterizations, page turner pacing, evocative and moving scenes written with heart and language that is both fresh and entertaining.

—Mesa, Arizona
September, 2022

The Deadly Pay-Off
William H. Duhart

For my Mother and Father
with my deepest affection and gratitude

Chapter One

Trouble was in his apartment. It had awakened him, a sound, a scent—something. Tank Tabor could feel it, slithering around the lower part of his belly, up and down his spine; the prickle of danger. Somebody besides himself was there, and nobody was supposed to be—not since the choice flesh that lived in the next apartment had wiggled out an hour before dawn, her fifty-buck fee well earned.

A thin slice of Milwaukee's summer sunlight burned the back of one of Tabor's big hands. Out of the corner of one eye he saw a spot of the startlingly white marble façade of the Carlton Hotel across Wells Street through the green slats of the partially drawn Venetian blinds. He rolled one eye up toward the small electric clock on the bedside table. The clock told him it was noon and a factory whistle bellowing far across town agreed.

He lay there in bed in his pajama bottom, straining his ears, trying hard to keep his eyelids from flickering. His six-four two-hundred-pound frame was motionless, the rank taste of the juice he'd swilled last night still strong in his mouth. Every cell of his brain began to churn. They were grinding out the danger signals, he thought. When you're fairly well acquainted with more than a few of the sins of the world and make your living gambling with hoods, you develop a sharp sense of danger.

The whistle stopped bawling, and the only sounds he could hear came from the city outside: the hum of swiftly moving traffic along the walk, a car door slamming, the short rapid clicking of a babe's spike heels against the pavement.

He was debating whether he should get up when an

oily voice in back of him said: "You can roll over and see your company now, Tank."

He did. The two gaily dressed gunsels were standing a little inside the doorway of his bedroom calmly watching him. He looked back at them, a scowl on his hard, handsome face. Offhand he couldn't think of the names they had been given at birth, but he knew they now answered to Trigger Slim and Moe. They were suspected of taking more than one poor slob for that long ride.

"There's a bell on my front door," Tank growled.

"Why take the fun out of it?" Trigger Slim asked in his oily voice, grinning.

"What the hell do you clowns want?"

"Moe, Tank sleeps with rocks in his dukes." Trigger's running-buddy didn't reply, just kept on staring at Tabor with his hand inside his screaming-pink sports jacket, quiet, motionless, Napoleon-style.

Without looking away, Trigger Slim held out a manicured hand and Moe shook a cigarette into the upturned palm. They made a hell-of-a-looking team, Tabor thought, as he sat on the edge of the bed, dragging his fingers through his wild tangle of dark hair. Trigger Slim with a lanky narrow body, a lot of round skull, and a chin like the bottom part of a nickel top; his running-buddy, Moe, just the opposite—a big monkey-faced lad with heavy, oily black hair and a set of generously muscled chops. In all the time Tabor had seen him around—at least eight or nine years—he'd never seen Moe smile nor heard him talk.

Trigger Slim lit his cigarette with a gold lighter and blew smoke toward Tabor's face. "Somebody wanna see you," he said, dropping the lighter into the coat pocket of his canary gabardine suit.

"Tell him I'm busy," Tabor yawned.

"It ain't a him."

Tabor got up and padded across the Chinese rug to get a smoke out of the pack on the wide mahogany dresser. He lit up with a kitchen match he found under an ashtray, noticing that the six-grand bankroll he carried around to gamble with was still intact. He wondered what the hell this was all about.

"Changed bosses, huh," he said, absently rolling the dead match stick between his fingers. "Last time I saw you two, you were lugging heaters for Arky Calahan."

"Arky's still boss," Trigger Slim told him. "Me and Moe, we're just doing like he said and running an errand for Kate Lamain—which is to see that you show at her pad this sunny P.M. Now on with the rags."

That stopped Tabor with the cigarette halfway to his mouth. Kate Lamain was a one-time good-loving girl of his. They were still friendly, so he couldn't understand her sending a pair of hoods after him. Why the hell was she hooked up with these bastards anyway?

"I can't figure you, Tank," Slim said, looking approvingly about the room. Tabor had a hotel-apartment, three modernly furnished first-floor corner rooms, overlooking the rich nightclub section of West Wells Street. For four years he'd lived there, getting up ten bucks a day for the place. At times he wondered if he wasn't a sucker for doing it, since he was now mostly sleeping by himself. He couldn't figure how that was worth ten greenies a day.

"You live in a castle," Slim said, the inspection over. "You sport suits that cost maybe a yard and a half, you're pushing a new convertible Caddy. Still you use them undersized logs to light your smokes. How come? That a new kick or something?"

"Saving dough," Tabor said through another yawn.

"A hustler saving bread. Never heard of it." Slim glided over to the dresser and smeared his cigarette stub over the bottom of the glass ashtray. "End of random conversation. Let's go."

"Told you I'm busy."

Tabor heard a nasty click and looked around. Moe had hauled out a piece of iron, a piece designed to eject six .45 slugs.

Kate Lamain's place was in Fox Point. It was a $95,000 eight-room bungalow of Lannon stone, set in the center of twenty acres of neatly barbed undulating grass and huge beds of creeping phlox and tulips and a multiflora rose fence. When Tank in his Caddy, closely followed by Trigger Slim and Moe in their long black Buick, turned onto the macadam that coiled through the grounds, they saw Kate in back, beautifully poised on the high dive of her enormous pool. The green Bikini she wore would have made a snake dancer's G-string look like a pair of Italian pantaloons. She waved for them to come on over and drifted off the board into a perfect swan. Tabor ogled at her full glistening thighs until she sliced the surface of the water.

"A goodie," Trigger Slim said.

"Yeah," Tabor agreed.

He parked beside the house. Moe pulled the Buick sedan close up behind the Caddy and they got out and walked toward the pool. It was three o'clock and scorching hot. The sky-blue sharkskin that housed Tabor's body was supposed to be ideal for summer—or so his tailor had told him—but today it felt like a steam-heated space suit.

Kate climbed from the pool, all brown and curvy and glistening with suntan lotion and droplets of water. She was brown-eyed and honey-haired and her soft, golden body was rich with the right kind of curves.

"Hello, darling," she greeted Tabor, removing her green bathing cap. "You boys can leave him with me now."

Slim turned and went back toward the house, with Monkey Face Moe trailing after him like a trained ape.

Kate gave Tabor a dimpled, white-toothed grin and then fluffed her shoulder-length hair. She picked up a green Turkish towel from the edge of the pool and patted at her face.

"Darn it, you big baboon, don't just stand there glaring at me."

"Why'd you send those clowns after me?"

"That was the only sure way I knew of getting you out here. Since you stopped sharing the bed, asking you to come out hasn't done any good."

She gave him the towel and turned around. He dried her golden back as he always used to do when they were together. In Milwaukee Kate was the queen of the good-time girls. It was known that on one occasion she had received an ocean-going yacht in return for a week end of her good-loving. As Tabor felt the softness of her sleek body beneath his hands he decided she hadn't lost an ounce of her yacht-producing potential. He tightened up, fighting for control. It was a hell of a rumble. He wasn't helped any by the luscious scent of My Sin floating up from her hair.

"Darling," Kate said, "it's terribly important or I wouldn't have sent them." She took the towel from him. "Let's get out of this sun."

He followed her to the patio, breathing deeply of the flower-scented air and watching her lively rear action. In the shade of the patio he dropped into a lounging chair, and knuckled the Panama to the back of his head. Kate laid the towel on the wrought-iron table and went to the portable bar in the corner. Inside the house, Sarah Vaughan's recording of "Make Yourself Comfortable" was easing from the record player. Tabor's gaze stayed on Kate as she went about the business of mixing drinks. She was going at it too slow and he realized, for some reason, she was stalling. He settled back. Long ago, when they were kids, he had learned it was a waste of energy to try to get her to give before she was ready to.

She laughed softly, an impish, tinkling sound. He raised his head and saw her looking at him, smiling knowingly. She brought him a highball and stretched out on a lounging chair beside him.

"You miss what I used to put on you, don't you?" she said.

"It was nice."

She reached over and eased her hand up and down the inside of his thigh. "Why don't you come back into the fold? We could go to Superior and buy ourselves a mink ranch and forget this kind of life. I'm sick of it. Okay?"

"Uh-uh. We're too much alike. You want to boss and I've never learned to be led."

Her fingers were like live wires on his thigh. Everything in him tingled. Another rub or two and he'd be panting like an overheated pup.

"You could make me what you want," Kate said, looking soberly up at him. "Anything. And you know it."

He took a sip of his highball and shook his head. He knew she meant it; that's what hurt. He felt sorry for her. But she didn't want pity from him, not without an overtone of love. It had started a long time ago. When they were kids Kate was the girl downstairs in the first floor front, and he was the boy on the third floor rear who had an appreciative eye for beauty and a ready story. He started feeding his story to her on their stoop one summer night and wound it up in a dingy buck-fifty hotel room. To him Kate had been a momentary necessity, but for her it had been love and still was. He'd never stopped feeling like a heel's heel for having fed her a line and beaten her for her virginity.

He tasted the highball again and shifted the talk into a different groove. "What's all the important news?"

"Arky Calahan's on his way out. I don't know exactly what he wants. But I'll tell you this much—he doesn't forget anybody who does him a favor."

His eyebrows went up questioningly. "What kind of favor?" he asked quietly, wondering what Arky Calahan could want. Calahan was the top dog. He bossed every racket in the city.

Kate shook her head. "Let Arky tell you. Of course it's nothing you can't handle. And it's a chance for you to get tight with him."

"Who said I wanted to get tight with him? Maybe I like playing solo."

She took her hand from his thigh, drew her leg up in the seat. He enjoyed the glistening picture it made.

"Heck, Tank, how long do you think you can go on the way you've been winning from the boys?" she asked with an impatient gesture. "The word's already out on you. Luke's telling it around that you shot him a hand in a poker game at Frank's last week and took him for twenty thousand."

His voice was quiet. "You believe that?"

"Now don't get that temper of yours up. I'm merely pulling your coattail. I know darn well you've never cheated anybody in your life. That is," she amended, giving him a wistful smile, "not gambling, anyway. Still, the kind of talk Luke's putting out isn't doing you any good. A little more of it and soon you won't be able to sit in on a game in Milwaukee."

"Maybe not, but I won't worry about it."

"The thing to do," Kate went on, "if you want to keep on sitting in on their games, is to get with the bosses of the city, become one of them. That way you'll at least have the protection of an organization, and you won't be a target for every thug in town."

Tabor shook his glass, watched the cocktail bead, then level off again.

"When it gets so I'll have to hook up with a mob in order to gamble, I'll square up. Get into some legitimate business."

Kate absently rotated her glass with the palms of her hands, looking off into space, frowning slightly. He drained his glass and took a deep breath of the hot, perfumed air while the whiskey-heavy drink burned his throat.

Kate took his glass, gave him hers, saying, "Organization's the thing, Tank. You can't get around it."

He shrugged. "Maybe."

Out front a car door slammed, and a moment later Arky Calahan pushed open the screen door and stepped out onto the patio.

"Hello, Kate, Tank," he said. He spoke around a chewed-up cigar butt.

"Hello, Arky," Kate said.

Tabor nodded. He sipped at Kate's highball, watching Calahan closely as he lowered himself to the edge of a chaise longue.

Calahan was middle-aged and built like a boxcar—flat-featured and wide. He had bushy red hair and a concrete chin that jutted out under a pair of healthy cynically twisted lips. He didn't look the part of a powerful racket boss, Tabor thought. He ordered his suits out of a mail-order catalog. He rode around in a two-year-old Chev and smoked cigars that smelled like baked rubber, but he was the boss. The boss of the sharpies. The boss of the rats. And the boss of dope and prostitution and every number wheel in the city. If he gave the word, every so-called independent hustler would be smashed before morning.

Tabor looked away from Calahan when another man came from the house to lean against the door—a powerfully built young man with a rough, shadowed face and watchful, pig-like eyes. He answered to the name of Croaker and was Calahan's watchdog. He was a lad who liked to brag to his pals about how he'd slapped his widowed mother around and made her spend one of her old-age pension checks to buy him his first heater.

"Drink, Arky?" Kate asked, ignoring Croaker.

Calahan shook his head and centered his attention on Tabor. "I'll get right to the point, Tank," he said. "Your kid brother's out of line. He's working on a case that the coroner's jury labeled 'accidental death.' I want him to get off of it. He's the only private cop I couldn't talk into leaving the case alone. There's no profit in the thing for him, Tank, and I want him to leave it alone. You get me?"

"Not all of you," Tabor said quietly. "Give me more."

"That's all you need to know." Calahan looked a little surprised. There were never any whys about what he said. He insisted on prompt action and no fat-mouthing. "I want your brother to stop snooping. So you talk to him. Tell him he's way off course."

Tabor stared back at Calahan. This was the game, he thought. Somebody was always trying to uncover somebody else's trash. Now it was his kid brother Bill digging in Calahan's backyard. The kid sure as hell didn't know how to pick his people. He had climbed up on a guy's back who, with just a nod, could have him turned into cemetery feed in no time flat.

"Well?" Calahan said impatiently.

"I want to know the full score before I make a deal," Tabor answered calmly.

"Who said anything about you making a deal?" Annoyance edged Calahan's voice. "You're just looking out for your brother."

"I still want to know what's happening," Tabor insisted, his voice still quiet. "I don't walk into anything blind."

The record player cut off and there was a sudden delicate silence around them. Kate and Croaker watched them, the latter absently fingering a toothpick in his fat mouth. Tabor sipped the highball, unconcerned about the way Calahan's lips had flattened out.

Calahan was quiet a long time, carefully studying him. Finally he said, "Tess Andrews' husband, Ritchie, stepped out in front of a car and got himself killed. That was six months back. At the time of his death he was on my payroll. Coroner's jury ruled it 'accidental death' like I told you. But Tess is acting like a fool and saying it was murder." He paused to crank up a cigarette lighter that had a flame like a blow torch. He held his head to one side, struck the flame to the cigar butt. "Of course it wasn't murder," he went on, snapping the cover on the lighter. "Like the jury ruled, Ritchie's death was just accidental. That's all it was, an *accident,* and none of the snoops Tess Andrews hires can make anything else out of it. Thing is, I don't want them trying, don't want them prowling around my friends asking silly questions about me."

He paused, snapping the cover of his cigarette lighter open and shut, looking hard at Tabor through the bluish-gray puffs of smoke slanting across his flat features. Then he said abruptly; "Your brother's been asking several people I know a lot of questions about my past. Even told some of them he knew I had one of my boys murder Ritchie. That's foolish talk for your brother to be making. Murder's too serious a word for him to be connecting me with it so carelessly. I don't like it. I don't like it at all. So, Tank, you tell your brother to behave himself. That's the story. Now get on it."

Tess Andrews. Tabor said the name over and over to himself. The memory was distant and dim, but not quite forgotten. When Calahan mentioned her name, that old yearning had flared up in him again. He forced himself to stop thinking about her, telling himself it was over. He knocked off the rest of the highball and set the glass down on the floor. Yeah, it was over, he thought. Maybe not forgotten, but definitely over.

Calahan said, "Tank, I want to do this without trouble." He took the chewed-up cigar out of his mouth, then added: "If possible."

Tabor hesitated. "Okay, Arky. I'll see my brother."

"You do that, Tank. Today. Tell him I'll double whatever Tess Andrews is paying him and I want to know his answer before morning. I'll be here until ten."

"Okay, Arky."

Kate walked around the house with Tabor, holding on to his arm. They were almost to the car when she stopped to pull him around to face her. In her lovely bright eyes was a little girl's plea to be understood.

"Tank?"

"Yeah," he said coldly. "Give me the story now. Tell me you don't have anything to do with this deal."

"I don't," she said, shaking her head. "I heard about it from Trigger Slim. He told me Arky was going to push Bill and I knew you wouldn't stand for that. No matter how many guns Arky has on his payroll. To prevent trouble, I called Arky and told him you could work on Bill and straighten things out peacefully. That's all I did."

He pulled her to him, inhaling the bouquet of the perfume in her hair and brushed his lips across hers, gently. This was the way they'd always let each other know everything was all right between them again after a misunderstanding. No words. Just a kiss, and a smile.

"You still have the key to my door?" Kate asked afterwards, smiling.

"Uh-huh."

"Well, I'm still sleeping by myself and I haven't changed the locks on the place."

He grinned, patted her where her bathing suit bulged the most and turned away.

"Tank."

He paused, looked back over his shoulder.

"You haven't gotten over Tess yet, have you? You still love her." There was no jealousy in her voice, just despair.

"I don't want to talk about that, girlfriend."

Chapter Two

Fifty minutes after leaving Kate's place, Tabor was reluctantly climbing the stairs that led to Bill's third-floor office. The narrow hallway was dim and suffocating with the scent of cigar smoke and fresh paint. Tank took his time going up, thinking about Bill, about how they'd been separated twenty-one years ago, when he was thirteen and Bill nine, after Mom and Dad were killed. Thinking about it still made him feel lonely. The folks hadn't had much of anything but love to give him and Bill. Then even that had been taken away, cut off sharply by a gas-happy driver.

It had been the turning point in his life, perhaps in Bill's too. Right after Mom and Dad's funeral, Bill had been adopted by a wealthy couple, nice people who later had a bit of nasty luck with their investments. Tabor had been too big by then, so he was whizzed into an orphanage, a major manufacturing center of punks, perverts and thugs.

After six weeks in that weird establishment he was a snarling beast. On his first night there, Jager, a husky sixteen-year-old hooligan—a juicy-lipped bastard with a nasty right cross and a passion for the younger boys—had crept down from his end of the long dormitory after lights-out and run his hand under the blanket on Tabor's cot. He'd mumbled wetly in his ear: "My pride an' joy's a cute fat boy. Know what I mean, kiddo?" It took four of the other boys, bug-eyed with fright at what they were witnessing, to unclamp Tabor's hands from around Jager's neck. After that, until Jager was sent out to one of the farms five months later, Tabor had got in the habit of sleeping on his back with one hand knotted into a fist and the other gripping a length of lead pipe. It had been a cheery life.

Two years of that gentle life had been all he'd been able to digest. One fall night when it was raining up a storm he crawled out on the ledge of a dormitory window, slid down the drain pipe into the playground and scaled the medium-high wire fence around it. He took off like he was hot-footing after a fleet twenty-two-year-old virgin. He'd headed for nowhere in particular, saying over and over to himself that he'd rather die the death of a mongrel dog than let them take him back. He knew he'd have to walk light till his eighteenth birthday, the age at which the State Welfare Department figured you were old enough to go for yourself. He ought to make it; he was big enough to pass for eighteen.

He'd roamed from state to state, doing odd jobs, bell-hopping, gandy-dancing, dishwashing, never staying anywhere very long, always fearing that a piece of law was going to reach out and clamp a hand on his shoulder.

Then one cheerless morning over in Chicago, when he'd been out of the orphanage little better than a year and out of a job for more than a month, he was loafing around the South Water Produce Market. He was waiting for a fat slob in a grimy blue-striped apron to look the other way so he could snatch a couple of cantaloupes off his truck, when a lot of shiny black Chryslers pulled up to the curb about five feet from where he was standing. A squatty middle-aged man with bushy eyebrows got out of the car, turning up the collar of his expensive overcoat. Tabor knew the man from seeing pictures of him in the newspapers and the newsreels. The man was Steve Novack, Mr. Big of the rackets throughout Illinois and Wisconsin.

Tabor was all set to put the beg on the racketeer for enough money to get a Dutch lunch when he saw, from the corner of his eye, another car cruising toward them. A sleek black job with two guys in it who had the brims of their fedoras pulled low over their faces. He saw something else that jerked his head up.

The man on the inside had one of his arms poking through the window of the car, pointing at Steve Novack's unsuspecting back with a big gun.

Tabor didn't take time to think of what he was doing. One second he'd been rooted to the sidewalk gaping at the cannon in the guy's duke, then the next thing he knew he was hitting Steve Novack with a flying tackle, shouting: "Look out! Duck!"

As they jarred against the pavement, the gun cracked twice, the bullets whining past them and shattering the plate glass of the fruit market. They scuffled up close to Novack's car. But no more shots came. The gunsel's car hadn't stopped. Over his ragged breathing, Tabor could hear the car's powerful motor growling loudly as it picked up speed, quitting the scene.

They climbed up off the sidewalk. People from the produce stores were pouring out onto the street, crowding around them, gesturing and talking excitedly. Steve Novack held out a big-knuckled hand to him and Tabor shook it.

"Thanks, keed," Steve said. "Let's get out of this mob." They got into the Chrysler. Steve leaned across Tabor's knees and hollered out to one of the men in the crowd. "It's all right, Jerry. I take care of the window."

"Don't worry about the window, Steve," a huge red-nosed man yelled back, shaking his head vigorously. "Just you take care of your health. Them bastards won't miss forever."

Steve gave the man a short salute, then started the

car and pulled off, driving slowly. For several blocks they rode in silence, Steve's bushy brows drawn together with thought and Tabor's belly hurting like hell with hunger cramps.

Then, as he tooled the Chrysler onto Washington Boulevard, Steve said, "You save my life, fellow."

"That happen often?" Tabor asked. The cozy warmth of the big car had him blinking to stay awake. "I mean getting shot at."

"Two time, so far. Two time too many. I'm getting too old to be hitting the cement so hard like you throw me." Steve glanced at him, his wide mouth open in a grin, his strong white teeth sparkling. "You look hungry, kid," he said. "Stay with me and you live good." The big Chrysler purred ahead.

And Tabor lived good. With Steve he learned to love cards, good food, golf, music, baseball, clothes, bawdy humor—and the soft warmth of a mature woman's body.

The slamming of a door down the hall jerked Tabor from the past. He stepped into Bill's office and looked around, frowning at what he saw. The office didn't have much on a telephone booth, a couple of cracked windows was about all. It was choked with a banged-up wooden desk, a straight-back chair and a stingy bench. There was nobody in sight, but he heard grease popping in the back and smelled coffee brewing. The kid still couldn't afford to eat out, he thought.

He took in a long breath of the hot coffee-scented air and walked over to the window behind the desk. Standing there, the rest of the years tumbled by in a rush. And the thought of how long he'd been on the hustle suddenly made him feel weary. Except for the hitch he'd served in the Army during World War II—

a year in the States and two and a half years in China, Burma and India—he'd been leaning over crap layouts or card tables almost every day for the past seventeen years.

He cut off his sigh as Bill came into the ratty office, lighting a cigarette. He saw Tabor and paused. Then Bill smiled slowly, and shook hands.

"You're looking great, boy," Tabor said. At twenty-nine his brother still looked like the basketball star he had been at college, tall, but not quite so tall as Tabor, and slender. The dark brown suit he wore was a bit shiny and lighter in spots from many cleanings, but was neatly pressed. "How's the family?"

"Swell," Bill said, and Tabor could see his chest expand with pride. "Ruthie and the kids keep asking about you."

He went around his desk to a swivel chair that protested loudly when he sat down. "What's on your mind, Tank?"

Tabor parked a hip on the corner of the desk, took time to light a cigarette, and then said easily, "The Andrews case."

Bill looked at him, the cigarette, halfway to his mouth, forgotten. "What about the Andrews case?" he said slowly.

"Leave it alone."

A faint frown began inching over Bill's tanned face. It was evident he wasn't going to go for this without a rumble. "What the hell, Tank," he said. "What the hell."

"Stop working on the Ritchie Andrews case," Tabor told him, fixing him with a direct look. "You're annoying Arky Calahan."

"I see," Bill said quietly. "He sent you to make me stop, is that it?"

"It's not quite like that," Tabor said. He'd started

this out all wrong. Should have eased into the kid, but it was too late now.

"I think it is." Bill sat up stiff, studying his face. "Somehow Arky Calahan's found out that I know Ritchie was no hit-and-run victim but was murdered on his orders. Perhaps he knows I'll find out why he had Ritchie killed before the day's over. And since you're my big tough brother, he sent you to stop me before I drape a charge of first-degree murder around his neck. I suppose he thinks I'll bow out quietly? Just because you're one of them?"

"I don't know what he thinks. But I know the case is too far out for you." Tabor felt his own nerves getting tight. "Look," he said, struggling to hold down his temper, "before you push a guy like Calahan think about your family."

Bill leaned forward in his chair, his lean body taut. "What about my family?"

"Ruthie's young and pretty." Tabor reached over and took the forgotten cigarette from between his brother's fingers and snuffed it out in the large brass ashtray on the desk. "You want her to be a widow? And Bobby and Jane. Want them to be fatherless? Wake up, Bill. Arky Calahan's no play-pretty."

"I suppose he'll send you to pull the trigger when it's time for me to go?" Bill said. His eyes were puzzled and hurt. "How can you stay with such a filthy bunch of cruds?"

"I was brought up with cruds," Tabor said. "And if you don't know it, those cruds run the city."

"Well, you don't have to be scummy just because somebody else wants to be that way," Bill argued. "I think you like it. You should start going to church, Tank."

"Stop talking like a clown. Look, I didn't come here to argue." Tabor felt anger pushing hard at his control and mashed out his cigarette slowly, to give himself time to cool off. "I didn't want to come. But I'm here and it's for your own good. So stop trying to change me and listen to what I got to say."

He paused and stood up, looking down at the mixture of frustration and hurt in his brother's eyes. "This is Calahan's city, Bill, his jungle. You can't beat him so get up off him."

"You want me to run and hide?" Bill asked, his chest rising and falling rapidly. "You want me to pretend that I don't know Arky Calahan had Ritchie crushed like a cockroach? Is that what you want, Tank?"

"I want you to stay alive, that's all."

Bill leaned back in the chair, shaking his head slowly. "Tank, I'm not going to do it. There's still some law in this city."

"Don't talk to me about the law in this town! I know the law around here." Tabor jammed his big-knuckled hands down into his trouser pockets. This was worse than he had thought. The kid didn't even know how to wipe his own nose good. The law in this city! He wanted to laugh. Only there wasn't a damn thing funny about it.

He looked at Bill. "Go downtown and pick out every cop you think is on the square. Then around the first of the month go out to the parking lot behind Calahan's bar. You'll see most of them park their cars there. Then they'll go down the block to a respectable restaurant and hustle coffee, and when they get back to their cars they'll find neat little packages inside. With the compliments of Arky Calahan. That's your police force. So don't tell me about the law in this town."

"There are some honest policemen on the force."

"Sure," Tabor admitted. "But how're you going to tell who's who? Make a beef to a wrongo and you might as well have beefed to Calahan."

Bill shoved his fingers slowly through his curly brown hair. "I'm not going to give up the case. Once I start taking orders from crumbs I might as well turn in my license and tell my family I'm a crook." He shook his head angrily. "You'd better go, too. Because as long as you're with them you're against me."

Tabor's face hardened. "You're a fool," he snapped. "A hard-headed, educated fool. The only reason Calahan didn't goof you was because Kate Lamain begged him to give me a chance to talk to you. They'll kill you if you don't listen."

"I'll take my chances," Bill said.

He realized Bill had made up his mind but he had to try again. He knew what Calahan had meant when he said he wanted the thing done 'peacefully—if possible.' If not possible, Calahan would do it his way.

"Think about it, Bill," he said. "If it's money you need, I'll give you dough."

"There's nothing to think about. I'm not going to get off the case." Bill began to shuffle papers around on his desk, not looking at Tabor. "I don't need money. Not that kind, anyway. Now please leave, Tank. I have work to do."

Tabor hesitated, then turned and strode out of the office. When he hit the hallway he saw with a shock that Trigger Slim and Monkey Face Moe had tagged along behind him from Kate Lamain's place. They were leaning against opposite walls, not four feet from Bill's open office door.

"What do you clowns want?"

Slim slowly rubbed the side of his long chin, regarding him seriously. Moe's right hand was out of sight, under his left armpit. Tabor met his dull, stupid eyes.

"You got lice, fella?"

The big muscled-mouthed gunsel didn't even blink. Trigger Slim tilted his fat head toward Bill's office. "Didn't go so good in there, eh?"

"Everything's going to be all right."

"You might as well tell your friends the straight story, Tank."

His face stiff, Tabor turned and saw his brother in the doorway of his office. "Let me handle this, will you?"

Bill looked past him to Trigger Slim and Moe. "You crumbs can go back and tell Arky Calahan he can forget any ideas he has of making a deal with me. I don't deal with murderers."

The fool. Tabor cursed to himself. He came around to Trigger Slim and Moe again. Nothing had changed in their faces. The seconds trudged by. Trigger Slim, looking quietly at Bill, held out his hand to Moe and Moe dumped a cigarette into his palm with his free hand. His other hand was still buried under his left arm. Slim fired up the cigarette, uncoiled himself off the wall, cut a glance at his running-buddy, and jerked his head in the direction of the stairs. "Let's go."

Tabor watched them a moment, until they were well down the hall. Then he spoke to his brother. "Where's your heater?"

"At home. Why?"

"Better make wearing it a twenty-four-hour-a-day habit from now on," Tabor advised him. Then he followed Slim and Moe down the airless, dim-lit hall.

Out in the ninety-degree heat again he paused and wiped sweat from his face and neck and hands. The two gunsels were across the street climbing into the Buick. They were on their way to report back to Calahan.

That wasn't good. He motioned for the gunsels to hold up a minute.

"Look," he said, coming up to Slim on the driver's side of the car. "I can still kill this thing."

They gave him the dummy-style treatment, mouths closed, features relaxed, and looked at him with eyes that were as alive as rusty pop bottle tops.

"If nobody hires my brother," he plowed on, "he can't work the case. That's the law. I can get Tess Andrews to forget everything. That's just as good."

Trigger Slim stuck his arm out the window and thumped his cigarette butt at a black cocker spaniel puppy toddling across the street. He scored a hit with the live butt. Startled and frightened, the puppy yelped.

Trigger Slim chuckled and looked at Tabor again. "How you get that done's up to you. But Arky wants it done."

"I can do it," Tabor said, keeping his voice free of anger with much effort.

"You better get to getting then, Tank. You ain't got a thousand years."

Tabor nodded, then turned abruptly and went back to the other side of the street.

Inside the car, it was all he could do to light a cigarette. His hands were trembling for the first time in nearly ten years.

He wanted to kill Trigger Slim.

He started the car and rolled away from the curb. In the rearview mirror he saw the gunsels drive to the opposite corner and make a left turn. He wasn't rid of the bastards. They'd be around.

He junked his half-smoked cigarette, blinked sweat out of his eyes, and yanked his shirt open at the collar. Then he got to thinking about Tess. That was hard. Not just thinking about her, but trying to do it objectively, as if she represented nothing more than a necessary connection, one he had to make in order to keep Calahan from killing Bill. He still remembered that ten years ago she had been his babe, the love of his life, with all the trimmings. At least he'd thought she was his girl until he came home from an eighteen-month stay in a Japanese prison camp and caught her on her back, looking over a jodie's shoulder, with nothing covering her writhing body but him and perspiration.

He fired up another cigarette. Dragging on it, he let the smoke trickle from his nose, thinking of how that scene was supposed to have deadened everything he'd ever felt for Tess. It hadn't though. He knew that now, but nobody could have made him admit it.

Chapter Three

It was five after six when Tabor parked before Tess's apartment house, an expensive ten-story building on the far north side of town.

He got out and walked up the gleaming canopied entrance, feeling strange about the visit. It was going against the promise he'd made himself; never to come back. But he couldn't let that stand in his way now. As Trigger Slim had said, Calahan wanted to know Bill's answer—before morning.

He pushed the bell to Tess's apartment and waited, impatience rising in him now. He took a long drag on the crumpled cigarette butt and mashed it out in the sand urn beside the door. After two more tries at the bell, the door buzzed and he pushed it open, then took the self-service elevator up to Tess's fourth-floor apartment.

Tess was waiting in her doorway. She looked at him, standing easy, her big blue eyes neither friendly nor unfriendly. She hadn't changed much in the ten years he hadn't seen her, he thought, looking at her sandy hair, still curly and cut short, and at the lush lines of her full ripe body showing through the thin oriental-designed pajamas and robe she wore. A little older; a lot lovelier.

"Come in, Tank," she said finally, breaking a several second silence. "Bill called and told me to expect you."

"He tell you what I want?" Tabor asked, following her into the apartment and closing the door. Her voice still had the soft richness in it that used to move him so. It still made him feel more than a finger of desire. He struggled to keep it down.

"No," Tess said, "but he told me not to do it. Whatever it is."

"I see." He stopped in the center of the deep-napped rug and looked about approvingly. The room was large and high-ceilinged, with a long picture window hung with curtains of iridescent material that changed colors whenever a small electric fan on a low white oak table whirred their way. A plush oyster-white sectional sofa and deep chairs and several soft pillows about the floor made the room like Tess—luxurious and beautiful.

"What is it you want, Tank?" Tess was sitting on the sofa with her big-calved legs close together and stretched out in front of her. Her hands were pushed down into the deep pockets of her robe. She watched him impersonally, her full red lips faintly puckered.

"It's about Bill," he said. He put the Panama on a pink pillow and sat down in a deep chair across from Tess, breathing in her tantalizing perfume. "I want you to tell him to stop investigating your husband's death."

Thin eyebrows went up. She gave him a long level questioning stare from her big blue eyes.

"That's an odd request."

Tabor dipped his chin at her. "I know," he said, and leaned forward in the chair. "I want you to do it just the same. And tonight."

"Why should I fire Bill?" There was a touch of color in her cheeks. She crossed her knees. They were beautiful knees, dimpled and smooth. A picture of them came into his mind as he'd last seen them and he began to burn inside. But he kept his face expressionless.

"Just fire him," he said. "That's all."

"Don't you think you're being high-handed," she said coldly, "coming here ordering me to do something without giving me any explanation?"

"I think it's best you not know why. Maybe then you'll stop trying to dig up a lot of grief for yourself."

"And just who, may I ask, decides what's best for me?" She pushed back her hair with an irritable flick of her hand.

"Okay, okay," Tabor growled, nodding and motioning with his hand. "Don't blow a fuse. It's like this. The investigation's annoying Arky Calahan. He wants it stopped. Now. If you don't fire Bill and make him quit the case, Calahan'll do it. Bill can't stand up under the kind of pressure Calahan'll put on him. That's the way the story goes."

"Then Ritchie *was* murdered," Tess said slowly, studying him more carefully now. "Where do you fit into this, Tank?"

"I'm just a runner. Calahan's just giving me a chance to talk some sense into Bill's head."

"How generous they've become," Tess said, with a sharp twist of her lip. "Ritchie didn't get a warning. They just shoved him in front of a car and forgot about it. But then my husband didn't have a brother on Arky Calahan's payroll."

"Look," Tabor said impatiently. "I didn't come here

to discuss how Ritchie got wasted. I just don't want the same thing happening to Bill. Will you fire him?"

"What did Bill say?"

"Bill's a fool. He's been influenced by too many movie detectives."

Tess looked at him a long time with her ripe red lips slightly parted. "My husband was murdered. And Arky Calahan murdered him," Tess said tensely, leaning toward him, her eyes smoky with anger. She stood up suddenly, crossed her arms over her proud breasts, and gripped her shoulders as though trying to pull them together. She paced the length of the large room several times, her footfalls silent in the deep-napped rug. Then she came back and faced him again. "If Bill wants to quit, that's all right," she said, her voice changed back now to its usual softness. "I wouldn't want him to get into trouble."

"Call him and tell him he's fired."

"Apparently you don't know your brother very well. Regardless of what I tell him he won't let the likes of Arky Calahan boss him around. He's not like you. When he called he said he would continue on the case whether I want him to or not. Said he had to stay on it now."

"You're lying," Tabor said sharply, sitting up straight with sudden fear clutching at his gut. But he didn't believe the words as soon as they left his mouth. Thinking back rapidly, he couldn't recall Tess ever having told him a lie about a serious matter.

Watching her smooth face, he came up out of the chair. "Call Bill," he said roughly, gripping her shoulders and turning her toward the phone. "Let me hear you tell him he's fired."

Tess jerked away from him and swung around, her chin stiff. That smoky look was back in her eyes again but when she spoke her voice was so low he could barely hear it.

"Keep your hands off me. And don't tell me what to do."

"I'll tell you this," said Tabor, "you and Bill are campaigning for plots in some cemetery. Calahan's big business, in case you didn't know. He's got judges, lawyers, cops, aldermen, and a boatload of lesser so-called solid citizens in his corner. His take-home pay from the dope dealers, bookies, thrill-peddlers, and bootleggers runs into the millions. What's more, he didn't get a stranglehold on the rackets by following the golden rule. And if you think he's going to just look on while you and Bill light a fire under his rear, you both should be committed to a cell with padded walls.

"Ritchie's dead. He wasn't worth a damn when he was alive. So what if he did get washed away? He was all the time begging for it."

"That isn't true!" Tess said through her teeth. Her breasts, rising and falling quickly, pushed hard at her crossed arms, and the veins in the backs of her hands stood out like thick pieces of white string. "Ritchie was good to me. Good to everybody. You're talking this way because I married him and you're jealous."

Tabor grunted nastily, to hide the hurt her words made him feel. "Your husband was a clown and a cheese-eater. I know of two guys he ratted on. Guys he'd been breaking bread with. One burned and the other got life. So don't run off at the mouth to me about that punk's virtues. Just get on that phone and call Bill and tell him he's fired."

She tossed her head angrily and opened her mouth as the phone jangled. She went down the room to an ivory telephone sitting on a shelf and lifted the receiver.

After saying hello, she listened a moment, then said,

"Yes, he's here. But I want to tell you something first. Stop investigating Ritchie's death. I don't want you to go on. No arguments, just let it drop." She looked around at Tabor, "Bill wants to talk to you."

He took the receiver out of her hand. "What'd you tell Tess?" he snapped into the mouthpiece.

"That I'm going to stay on the case," Bill answered coldly, "whether she wants me to or not. So you might as well let her alone and go back to Arky Calahan."

"Don't be a fool. Anyway, what the hell's happening between you two? Why're you so willing to get crushed for Tess? If she is warming your bed, those things don't get that good. Not good enough to commit suicide for."

"Tank," Bill said quietly, gently, "your mind is sick with filth. Get away from Arky Calahan and his kind. Tell you what, Tank. Come live with Ruthie and me for a while. What say?"

Tabor took a deep breath, then said in a controlled voice, "Listen, Bill, what you say is fine and I'd like nothing better. But if you don't wake up and get some fat on your head, you're not going to be shacking with Ruthie or anybody else. Now get this good, Arky—" The phone in his hand went dead with a click.

For a long moment he stood there, the receiver still up to his ear. The half-baked detective. What the hell could he be thinking about? Trying to smack down Calahan's setup solo. What the hell had Tess done to the kid? Or promised him?

He felt her watching him and spoke into the phone, to keep her from knowing Bill had been so emphatic. "Go home and think about it, eh, kid," he said easily. "Toss it around with Ruthie. She's levelheaded. See what she says ... Good. Give Ruthie and the kids my best. Speak to you later." He cradled the dead receiver.

When he turned around, Tess was standing beside

the sofa rubbing her cheeks slowly with her palms and watching him with something close to pity in her eyes.

"Tank," she said softly, "What's come over you. You've changed so ..."

"Don't give me that mother routine," he said in a hard voice, a mixture of anger and fear heavy in his big chest. "I don't need it and don't want to hear it. You had no business ever hiring Bill to buck Calahan. If Calahan gets to him I'm holding you responsible. Remember that." He got his hat from the pillow and moved to the door.

"I did what I could," Tess said in a little voice. "I fired him."

With his hand on the knob he looked over his shoulder at her. Her big blue eyes were troubled. "You better do more than that, baby," he told her evenly. "You better make damn sure it takes. Because if anything happens to him I'll break your beautiful neck."

He left her standing there, lovely and scared.

In the self-service elevator he got out a cigarette and a match. It took four tries before he could ignite the match with his thumbnail. It was like that whenever he was in a touchy, explosive mood. He left the elevator, thinking that he'd have to shoot Calahan a story, anything to get him to hold still until he could get Bill to come in. He couldn't afford to let Calahan know he hadn't got any favorable action.

Outside, he paused, breathing his cigarette smoke and trying to pick the flaws out of the story he was going to tell Calahan.

He flipped his cigarette stub across the wide sidewalk and stepped off the stoop.

The black Buick sedan was parked behind his car. Trigger Slim, his hat shoved back on his oversized cranium, a cigarette drooping from the corner of his thin lips, stood leaning back on the Buick's right front fender. Moe was inside the car, his dull eyes fixed in an unwavering stare on the canopied entrance of Tess's building.

Slim said, "How'd it go?"

"Nice," Tabor said. He stopped beside his car. "Real nice. Tess called my brother and fired him while I was up there."

Slim eyed him with a quiet level glance. "Maybe I better go up and have her call Arky and tell him the good news then." He pushed away from the Buick's fender and started for Tess's building. "Arky'd like to get good news right away."

Tabor moved in front of him, blocking his path. His face was stiff, his voice quiet, ominous. "Stay away from her. Now and always."

Still eyeing him quietly, Slim sucked on his cigarette and blew smoke in his face. "And I had you figured for a real down cookie. Now you're fouling up my good opinion of you by acting like a hood."

He shook his head sadly and went to go around him. Tabor grabbed the lapels of his coat and pulled. "I said stay away from her."

"Did you?" Slim's voice was like the silky hum of a well-oiled sewing machine. He flipped his cigarette out into the street. "Unhand the dry goods, Tank."

Tabor wanted to give up some more lip, but the click of the hammer going back on Moe's .45 sounded like the hike of a ratchet jack. The gun's bore peeping at him over the window ledge of the Buick looked a foot round.

He unhanded Slim's dry goods.

"Look," he said, "so it didn't go nice. That doesn't mean I can't get my brother off the case. All I need is a few more hours to work on him. He'll come in. I know he will."

With meticulous care Slim smoothed his coat lapels where Tabor had gripped them. "Your hands is sweaty, Tank," he said. "Sweaty and dirty." Turning, he went and got in the Buick.

"Look." Tabor strode over and leaned down to the window on Moe's side of the car, ignoring the yawning bore of the .45 the monkey-faced clown had an inch from his left eye. "You guys don't have to report to Calahan right now. Give me a little more time."

Slim said, "Arky told us to beat it back right away and if we don't, we'll be crossing him. You know for yourself, Tank, it takes a lot of nerve to cross a guy like Arky. I ain't got that much nerve."

Tabor said, "I'll mash a bill apiece on you boys."

Trigger Slim shook his head. "My nerves is real bad, Tank."

"Two bills apiece."

Slim nodded, pursing his thin lips. "What about vacation money? You know we'd have to cool it for a while."

Tabor said, "I'll sweeten it another bill."

"Now, Tank." Slim shook his head sadly. "You know that ain't the kind of bread me and Moe'll need." He held up his hand and shook it. "Looka there. Even just discussing crossing Arky, like gentlemen, got me going to pieces. It'll take a lot of traveling for me to get myself together after we cross him. At least three bills worth. And since me and Moe is aces, I gotta have him with me all the time. So he's gonna need three bills, too, plus another deuce for nerve treatment. Couldn't think of going without him."

"Five bills apiece?" Tabor growled. "I'm not financing you guys a trip to Mars."

"If we cross Arky, trying to get to Mars ain't gonna be a bad idea. It ain't that me and Moe's trying to squeeze you, Tank. Far be it from us to try poking one in you just because you're over that well-used barrel." He straightened under the wheel and wrinkled his face, trying to look scared. The expression was as phony as a young nympho's promise to never love again. "Maybe we oughta forget the whole thing. I—"

"Okay, okay," Tabor cut in. "We're dealing. How're we going to work this?"

Slim knuckled the side of his long chin, thinking. Finally he said, "Tank, just to make things look for real, I'd go on out and tell Arky my brother was gonna raise up off the case, if I was you. Me and Moe can yes for you. That way, Arky won't have no reason to get suspicious right away. If me and Moe don't show back in a little while, like he told us, he's gonna send somebody else to check on you."

That was a piece of good reasoning, Tabor decided. He nodded. "Okay, I'll mash the grand on you guys as soon as we get done talking to him."

"Mash it on us now."

"Later."

Slim twisted the key in the ignition, kicked over the motor. "You just lost two of the best yes men in the business."

"Wait a minute," Tabor said. "I'll straighten you now. Just don't get a head full of wrong ideas." There was nothing else he could do. He had to come in if he didn't want Bill to get washed away. Time was what he needed most and they could help him get a few more hours, at least three, anyway.

Wetting his thumb, Trigger Slim gave the money a double check, moving his almost meatless lips in a silent count with every flip of a bill. His eyes were shining like the headlights on a diesel locomotive on a moonless night. He thumbed off five bills, folded them, and slid them into Moe's shirt pocket. Moe didn't look around, just kept his eyes stuck in Tabor's direction. Pocketing his end of the squeeze money, Slim said, "We'll just tell Arky your brother wanted to argue, but you wouldn't listen to no argument and finally got him to come in. You know, just to make it sound pure. We won't mention the Tess Andrews dame."

Tabor told them that was real nice and stepped back from the car. They shot away from the curb, leaving behind twin trails of smoking rubber on the asphalt and the smell of cheap gas in the air.

Chapter Four

Tabor drove with the top down, and the breeze took some of the tightness out of him. Shadowy fingers of evening were creeping along the road as he wheeled the Caddy onto the macadam coiling through Kate Lamain's flower-heavy grounds. He saw the black Buick sedan parked alongside the house, braked to a stop behind it and got out. Nobody showed up out front so he strolled around Kate's luxurious rancho to the patio. Kate and Monkey Face Moe were the only two in sight.

"Make out all right, darling?" Kate asked. She had shed the scanty Bikini and donned a pea-green two-piece outfit with a pleated skirt that flared out beautifully. She was at the portable bar mixing drinks in a tall glass sweaty with frost. Moe sat hunched on the side of a chaise longue, his elbows on his heavy knees, a dying cigarette sagging from the corner of his muscled chops. He'd been X-raying Kate's fine parts but now he switched his interest to a spot between Tabor's eyes.

"Everything's real nice," Tabor told her. He lit a

cigarette, ignoring the blood-freak, and settled down in a cushioned chair by the wrought-iron table. "Where's Arky?"

"Inside," Kate said, nodding toward the screen door. "He heard you drive up and said he'd be right out. Want a drink?"

"Fine." The door opened, banging against the wall, and Tabor looked around. Calahan strode out onto the patio, followed by Trigger Slim.

Calahan said, "How did things go, Tank?"

"Nice," Tabor said. "All my brother needed was a little talking to."

Calahan plopped his boxcar frame into a chair, watching him narrowly.

"You're a liar."

Everybody froze—Slim and Moe, Kate at the bar, and Tabor, who had been about to drag on his cigarette. It was quiet enough to hear a mouse in tennis shoes tiptoe across medicated cotton.

Tank shot a glance at Trigger Slim sitting on the chaise longue with his running-buddy Moe. Slim met the nasty glance in his dummy-style—pop-bottle eyes, slack features. Moe followed suit.

"I didn't know you were silly, Tank," Calahan went on in a level voice. "You brought back a mouth full of lies and even tried to bribe Slim and Moe. Did you actually think ten dollars would make my boys cross me?"

Tabor stood up. He felt his scalp beginning to leak and shoved the Panama up off his forehead. Not only had Slim and Moe caught him over that well-used barrel and poked one in him, but had also broken it off up to the hub. And had made a grand doing it.

Kate put her back to the bar, moving slowly. Her eyes crinkled at the corners with incredulity. The tall glass in her hand shook noticeably.

"I had another gimmick I was going to use to make my brother come in," Tabor said. He knew he wasn't even conning himself. Calahan had caught him trying to sell him a snow job. But he had to say something, anything to get out from under this hammer. "I can still do it. All I need's a little more time."

Calahan's flat features showed nothing but their natural ugliness. He jabbed a ragged cigar butt into his face, cranked up his small-sized blow torch. Squinting slightly, he leaned his head to one side, brought up the lighter to the end of the cigar and looked at Tabor through the two-inch flame it threw off. Heavy smoke that smelled like baked rubber hid his eyes for a couple of seconds. Then he snapped the lighter shut and said: "A little more time for what? To manufacture a bigger lie?"

Tabor shook his head. His scalp was drowning but he didn't wipe. To get his back to the wall, he walked over beside the screen door and crushed the cigarette out in the ash stand that stood next to it. "I can still fix it. I—"

"You're through, Tank." Calahan's mouth flattened out. "You tried to play me for a fool. That was a mistake."

Tabor turned his head and saw Croaker, Calahan's big pig-eyed bodyguard, standing in the partially opened screen door. The door hadn't made a sound. That ever-present toothpick stuck out of Croaker's shadowed face and a giant-sized blue-steel automatic jutted out of his ham-like fist. Tabor wondered if it was the heater he'd slapped his widowed mother into buying with one of her old-age pension checks.

Calahan said, "Take him and smarten him up."

"No," Kate said, and came over and stood in front of Tabor. Her voice was quiet and steady although the skin over her raised cheekbones was taut. "Arky, why not give him more time to talk to his brother?"

Looking at her, Calahan puffed low-hanging clouds from the cigar butt. His anger had smashed his lips pancake flat, even where they curved around the cigar. His voice hadn't changed, was still level. "Croaker, smarten him up."

Kate backed into Tabor. Her hands gripped the legs of his pants. She smelled good, sweet and fresh. He put his hands on her shoulders, feeling the tension quitting his body and feeling his scalp drying up. He had control of himself now. He thought of making a try for Croaker but quickly rejected the idea. He couldn't chance getting Kate wasted. If he tried and missed and they killed him, they'd do her in to keep her from talking.

"Let me handle this, girlfriend," he said quietly. He guided her to a chair and forced her down into it. She gazed up at him and he turned away from the pain in her lovely brown eyes. "Okay, Croaker. Your play."

The toothpick jumping from one side of his mouth to the other, Croaker motioned him ahead with his automatic. "Over by the edge of the trees."

Calahan stood up, glanced at Trigger Slim and Moe. "Come along."

Tabor set a slow pace over the soft grass and they all headed for the trees, a thickly wooded area about two hundred yards from Kate's house. Nobody talked. Everything was breathless, waiting.

They halted and Croaker told Moe to cover Tabor. Then he backed Tabor against a tree, yanked his hands behind him, around the tree trunk, and snapped a pair of handcuffs on his wrists. Through the dusty evening shadows Tabor stared at Calahan's flat face. Calahan returned the stare, the abused cigar butt clamped in the side of his mouth. Someday he'd kill Arky Calahan, Tabor knew. There was no shaky fear inside him, only a slow-rising bitterness, a bitterness he had managed pretty much to control ever since he'd left the orphanage.

Croaker came around the tree and stood in front of him, his legs spread apart, his ham-like fists on his hips. He just stood there a while, his shadowed features immobile, staring him in the eyes. Then without even a flicker of warning he whipped a right to Tank's gut, brought it on up under his chin. The air left Tabor's lungs in a painful gush and his knees did a quick bend. The handcuffs chewed into his wrists as he sagged forward and his arms felt like they were coming out of their sockets.

Another blow to his chin snapped his head up and crashed it against the rough bark of the tree. The Panama flew off. He bit into his lip, trying to see through the haze that had settled down around his nose. All he could see was a lot of shadowy images resembling human beings doing crazy things, floating up and down and gliding round and round each other. There was a loud ringing in his ears. He shook his head. The ringing kept on.

Over the jangling he heard freakish giggling and knew he was giving up some blood somewhere. Moe, the gore-freak, was catching his jollies again.

After a few more headshakes Tabor's eyes settled in their sockets. All of them came into focus. But he didn't look at anybody but Croaker. The big bastard was still in front of him, a couple of feet away, grinning. Tabor got his feet under him and straightened up. Then he tried to geld Croaker with his right foot. Croaker let out a hoarse scream and doubled up, grabbing himself with both hands and squeezing his knees together. Tabor slashed out with the foot again, aiming for one pig-like eye with the point of his shoe. But Croaker was falling sideways and the side of the shoe barely grazed his left temple.

Tabor heard Calahan say, "Get him," and looked up to see Moe shuffling toward him, reversing the sawed-off .45 in his big fist. His giggles had his eyes almost shut. But he could see well enough to fake a blow at Tabor's nose with the gun and then clobber him with a left hand. The freakish giggling hadn't taken anything from his punching power, either. The left hand was a gut-buster.

Then Tank tried to do to Moe what he'd done to Croaker, but the play got him nothing except a headache. Moe side-stepped like a crafty, fast-moving heavyweight, and the shoe did nothing but churn the air and throw Tabor off balance. His big body shaking with shrill giggles, Moe waded in with the big-butted .45 raised, ready to crease his skull.

He creased it.

For a second or so Tabor's nerves were paralyzed. There was no pain. Nothing. Then his brain exploded into a thousand bright and painful lights that buckled his knees. He was nose deep in haze again. His breath was a ragged wheeze.

From somewhere on Mars came Kate's voice. It was soft. Not affectionately soft, but deadly soft. "Moe, don't hit him anymore."

A big quiet settled around them.

Breathing through his mouth, Tabor shook his head until the haze cleared. Then he saw Kate. She stood a little to one side of Calahan and Trigger Slim. There was a gun in her small fist, a man's gun, a snub-nosed .38, and she held it man-style, waist-high and steady. Her beautiful face was a mask of calmness. Everybody was staring at her but Croaker. He was knotted up on the ground moaning and still holding himself. Tabor wanted to say something, wanted to tell Kate not to get herself fouled up with Calahan. But he couldn't get a word through the pain inside him. All he could do was let out a weak croak.

"That's all, Moe," she said.

Calahan's teeth got a tighter grip on the cigar butt. "Who says so?"

"I do, Arky," Kate told him in that same soft voice slanting a glance at him. "Want to try to make a liar out of me?"

The silence held, stretched tighter.

Calahan chewed on his butt. Monkey Face Moe moved and Kate's voice whipped across the short space at him.

"Hold it! Under ordinary circumstances you might beat me, Moe. But your gun is backwards now and I'll send you to hell before you can get it around. So don't try it. Let it fall."

Moe was no mental Samson, but he had read the handwriting on the wall correctly and his .45 hit the ground with a soft thud.

Then Kate nodded at Trigger Slim. "Get those handcuffs off him."

Slim didn't move. He glanced at Calahan and rubbed the left side of his chin with the fingers of his right hand. Tabor called Kate but his voice was barely a whisper. He jerked his head violently, trying to warn her Slim was going to make a stab for the heater he always carried in a shoulder holster. Slim was fast, he knew, deadly fast. But Kate needed no telling.

A faint frown of annoyance on her face, she said, "Slim, if you even think what you're thinking now for a second longer, you won't be good for anything but fertilizer."

From the distance of ten or twelve feet Tabor saw Trigger Slim's lanky frame shiver as if somebody had dropped an ice cube down his back; then he literally snapped to attention, his arms stiff, tight against his sides.

Calahan said. "Let her have him, Slim. Get the keys to the cuffs off Croaker."

When Slim took the cuffs off, Tabor fell to his knees. Kate ordered Moe and Slim to take him to the house. She picked the Panama up off the ground and waited until Calahan got his bodyguard to his feet and then told them to walk ahead of her.

A few stars were out, looking like chipped diamonds in the belly of the sky. Darkness was dropping down fast and off in the distance, toward the city, Tabor could see a neon sign blinking its red and white eyes. By the time they were halfway back to the house he could walk on his pins unsupported. He staggered along like a wino who had just gutted a quart lacquer thinner can.

They stopped on the patio. Kate came around to Tabor and he took the snub-nose from her. The urge to do Calahan in was heavy inside him and Calahan sensed it too. His Adam's apple jumped up and down a couple of times and his flat face got shiny with sweat. But Tabor couldn't kill him, not in cold blood. He played the game hard, but not that hard.

He snatched Trigger Slim's and Croaker's heaters from their holsters and handed them back to Kate. "All right, Slim, you and Moe can tremble down the loot I gave you. All of it."

Simultaneously, the two gunsels flicked uneasy glances at Calahan. Then, avoiding his eyes, they dug into their pockets and brought up money. Tabor took it, gave it to Kate.

"See if it adds up to a thousand," he told her. "Your boys held out nine hundred and ninety greenies on you, Arky."

A moment later Kate said: "it adds."

He crammed the bills into his pocket then let his

gaze rest on Calahan. "Don't push my brother."

Calahan gave his cigar butt a long overdue break; he dropped it into the ashtray on the wrought-iron table. Looking up, he studied Tabor a while. "You say you can get your brother to play our way?"

He nodded.

Calahan said, "Let me know his answer tomorrow." He nodded at the heater in his fist. "Can we go?"

"Wait a minute." Tabor shifted the snub-nose to his left hand, then stepped up to Monkey Face Moe and tried to break him in two with a short hook to the belly. Moe blew out a big grunt, bent forward at the waist, and Tabor dropped him with a hook to his jaw that had every ounce of his thick shoulders behind it. The gunsel landed on his chin and slid three feet on the slick grass before he jack-knifed and toppled over on his side. He lay there thrashing his legs and trying to suck oxygen into his deflated lungs.

Tank stepped away. Throwing that last punch had let Tabor know his head hadn't stopped hurting. He swiped at the blood on the side of his face with his hand, nodded at Calahan. "I'll see you tomorrow, Arky. Slim, get your running-buddy up."

After Arky and his boys had left, Kate took him inside the house to her double-sized, blue-tiled bathroom and fussed over the crease in his skull. The wound wasn't bad, little more than a skin break. But it was a hell of a headache maker and his wrists burned. He splashed cold water over his face and hands.

Kate was sitting on the side of her pink bathtub. She crossed her legs, watching him worriedly. "Tank, you don't believe Arky was telling the truth about waiting until tomorrow for you to let him know Bill's answer, do you?"

"Why not?" he said, as he unplugged the sink and

sloshed water around in it. "A few hours more won't make any difference. All he wants is Bill off the case before he can bring up something that'll start the papers to blasting him and his political friends. That hasn't happened yet."

"Did you know that Bill is supposed to give the District Attorney some information on the case in the morning?"

"No. Who told you?"

"I overheard Calahan talking to Croaker about it after you left here this afternoon." Kate left her seat on the side of the bathtub. She had nice hip action, slow and snake-like. Coming up to him, she fluffed her glistening honey-colored hair, then took a towel and began drying his hands. "That's why I can't see Arky giving you until tomorrow to talk to Bill. If what I heard is true, tomorrow will be too late for you to do anything to help Arky."

"What do you think he's got in mind then?" Tabor asked, a feeling of dread beginning to bud in him.

Kate finished drying his hands and walked the length of her spotlessly clean bathroom to the long pink-curtained window that looked out over the swimming pool and the thickly wooded area beyond. Without turning from the window she said, "You know the way the game goes, Tank. What you can't control, you crush."

He got his jacket off the back of a chair, shrugged into it, and said, "Then you think Arky's trying to fake me off guard with this tomorrow business?"

Slowly she turned to face him. "I think Arky is going to try to hit Bill tonight. Maybe I'm wrong. But I don't think so."

He didn't think so, either. If Bill was going to give the D. A. some news about Ritchie Andrews' case in the morning, Calahan had to try to hit him tonight.

Mindful of the headache crease in his skull, he got his hat off the chair and eased it on his head. He walked up to Kate and pulled her to him. Her soft warm body melted into his, every wonderful line of it. She looked up at him, her moist red lips parted, her thoughts naked in her lovely eyes. There was a strong feeling for her deep inside him, but not deep enough. Kate would demand your whole love.

"Darling, what's the matter?" she asked softly.

He shook his head and put his hands on her shoulder. Then he touched her honey hair, the curve of her sun-browned neck, her smooth beautiful face, relishing the warm tantalizing smell of her. "Thanks for pulling me out from under that sap job."

The kiss was long and wet and when they came out of it they clung to each other, breathing hard and trembling. His hands shook uncontrollably.

With misty eyes Kate whispered, "You meant that as goodbye, didn't you, Tank? You're going to make Arky come by you to get to Bill, aren't you?"

"Get me those heaters I took off Trigger Slim and Croaker, will you, girlfriend?" he said.

Chapter Five

On the way to Bill's office, Tabor drove recklessly, weaving through the light traffic on Capital Drive at sixty miles an hour. He wheeled into Bill's block, and saw all of the windows of the office building were dark. He drove to a drugstore and called Bill's home. Ruthie, Bill's wife, answered. She told him Bill had left fifteen minutes ago, on his way to see Tess. They chatted a moment longer, talking about the kids, then exchanged goodbyes and hung up.

There wasn't much walking life along Tess's block,

just a pair of couples strolling hip-to-hip. A number of windows in Tess's building were bright with light and slow string music floated out to serenade the strollers. Tabor got out of the car and ambled through the canopied entrance. He sounded Tess's bell.

After a while her voice came through the speaker. "Who is it?"

"Tank. Bill up there?"

She hesitated, then said, "No."

"Look, Tess, if he's up there I want to know. Time's running out." He wondered where Bill was. Fear began to ride up and down his nerves.

"He's not up here," she said coldly.

"Well, let me come and wait for him. He told his wife he was coming here. Maybe we can stop him from getting his head blown off."

Nine or ten seconds jumped by. The heavy artillery in his back pockets had his pants sagging. He tightened his suspenders. Then the lock buzzed.

The apartment door was open when he got upstairs. Tess, wearing a brown gabardine robe, was curled up in a deep chair filing her fingernails. He leaned on the door and gazed at her curly sandy hair, remembering a few of the thousand-and-one little things he knew about her. The way her small feet turned in slightly when she walked, the shallow dimple that came into her unblemished cheeks when she smiled, the sensuous softness of her voice when she laughed. He fought against the yearning for her that come with the memories, telling himself to stop being a romantic clown.

Without raising her head Tess asked, "What did you mean when you said 'time is running out?'"

"I think Calahan intends to try to hit Bill tonight."

The nail file pressed down harder on the fingernail she was sawing on.

He said, "I think you're right about Ritchie having been murdered. At least Calahan makes me think so, the way he's hustling to keep anybody from investigating his death."

Tess looked up at him then. "I know Ritchie was murdered. At his inquest they said he had been drinking heavily. That was a lie. Ritchie hated anything that even had alcohol in it."

"Calahan ever say anything to you since Ritchie got killed?"

"Why, Tank?" Her voice was short and irritable. "You're not interested in how he died. You said so." Then she shook her head as if angry with herself for having steamed over. "Arky hasn't said anything to me himself, no." Her voice was calm now, soft. "However, two days before Ritchie was killed I came back from downtown and saw two of Arky's men leaving the building, and when I got upstairs I found the apartment had been searched. The locks on the front and back doors weren't broken or anything. But all of the closet doors were standing open and I knew I hadn't left them that way."

"Where was Ritchie? Maybe he left them open."

Tess shook her head. "Ritchie hadn't been home for better than two days. I don't know where he was. He didn't phone or send any messages to me. Next I heard, he was dead. When I learned of his death I was pretty sure he'd been in hiding during those few days and that the two men who'd searched the apartment had been looking for him then to murder him."

He nodded. "You're probably right."

"One of the men I saw leaving the building that time was the one you kept from coming up here today," she said softly, and her eyes were as soft and warm as her voice. "Thanks, Tank."

Tabor suddenly felt uncomfortable, exposed. He had

blown her out, had told her he'd break her pretty little neck, and then a few minutes later he'd been ready to go to war with Trigger Slim to keep him from talking to her. And she had picked up on all of it from her front window.

He searched her eyes for the laughter. There was none. She knew he was a fake, that he was still silly about her regardless of what he'd said and done, regardless of what she had done. So it was time for the big joke, the laughter. But instead of laughter, there was the same warm expression in her big blue eyes that he'd seen in Kate's a little while ago, just before they kissed. He didn't understand this.

Then the door chimes began acting up and he forgot about it.

Tess said, "That must be your brother. Push that button beside your head and let him up."

He reached up, knuckled a small black button on the wall below a brass mouthpiece, then straightened up and snicked the lock off the door.

A few seconds later he wished he'd left it locked.

Two tall men appeared in the doorway, hard-faced men whose beef could have been put to good use as line material on any of the pro football teams. They looked relaxed enough to be players, like they could move and hit if they had to. But they weren't athletes—they were plainclothes law. Tabor had seen them around town a number of times but didn't know their names.

"Tank Tabor?" the heavier piece of beef said. He looked as if he already knew the answer was yes.

He nodded.

"I'm Lieutenant Hacker, Robbery Detail," Big Beef went on, then indicated Less Beef with a tilt of his head. "This is Sergeant Jacoby. The Captain wants to see you downtown."

"For what?" Tabor asked quietly.

Big Beef casually slid back the right side of his jacket and just as casually clamped his big right hand around the butt of the nickel-plated .45 Colt that rested in a worn holster on his hip. "We got warrants for your arrest. Armed robbery and assault."

No expression crossed Tabor's features. But inside, his big chest was a cold knot of fear. Behind him Tess stirred. The two hunks of beef watched every breath he took. It wasn't necessary for him to hear any more of the story to know what it meant. This cute piece of fiction had first come to life among Calahan and his clowns and was meant to take him off the track so they could hit Bill without interference.

Big Beef stuck two pieces of yellow paper under his nose. "The warrants. This makes it all legal and proper."

The name on the warrant for armed robbery and assault was George Ackelforth. On the other warrant the complainant was a Horace Hensinfinger. He wallowed the names around in his head until they clicked into place and he realized how tight Calahan had fitted the frame around him. George Ackelforth and Monkey Face Moe breathed with the same pair of lungs. And the name Horace Hensinfinger belonged to his keen-chinned running-buddy, Trigger Slim.

Less Beef drew his heater, a .38 Colt automatic, and flicked the safety off. "C'mon, boy."

"Look, man," Tabor protested. "I didn't rob anybody."

"We didn't say you did," Less Beef told him. "We just gotta take you in because the captain handed us these warrants. Gonna shake him down up here, Lieutenant?"

"I'll get him."

Big Beef advanced toward him. Tabor knew they had him cold now. The two heaters in his hip pockets seemed to pick up weight with every step the big cop took. The thought of gambling on a surprise attack flashed through his mind but the readiness of the automatic in Less Beef's fist deadened the thought. He cut a glance back at Tess. She was staring at him, wide-eyed, perplexed and frightened.

"Look," he said suddenly, backing away from Big Beef. "Look, officers. This is all crazy. I haven't left this apartment for days."

"When you get downtown," Big Beef said, "tell it to the captain. Now be still."

Tabor ducked away from him again. "Wait a minute. Let's talk this over now."

Less Beef wagged his heater. "One more step, boy, and you answer to hop-a-long."

Tess's voice quivered across the room. "Tank, stop. He means it."

He stopped. The hard lines of Less Beef's face and his flame-bright eyes, narrowed now until they looked sleepy, told Tabor that Tess was right. The Lieutenant ordered him to turn his back and lock his hands on top of his head. When he did, the crease in his skull woke up again. Sweat poured into the wound.

The Lieutenant came up with the pair of heaters and Tabor heard Tess's sharp intake of breath. The apartment felt cold but Tabor knew the temperature hadn't changed. The cold was inside him, naked fear galloping up and down his taut nerves.

Big Beef stepped away from Tabor. "Well, well. A two-gun gent."

"Look," he said. Then he shut up. The cops were nothing but leg men carrying out orders. Beefing to them would get him nothing but a lot of stale gags. He did ask them how they had known to come there for him.

Keeping to one side, out of the path of the steady

automatic, Big Beef took the heaters to his partner and finished shaking Tabor down before he answered. Then, snapping a pair of steel bracelets on his wrists, he said, "That was easy. The guys that say you heisted them followed you here and called in to the station."

Less Beef flicked a glance at Tess. "What about her, Lieutenant?"

Looking down at Tess, Big Beef hiked up the front of his pants and then hunched his shoulders. "Nobody said nothing about her," he answered, and Tabor stopped holding his breath.

As the cops escorted him out of her apartment, he craned his neck around and hollered at her: "Don't forget what I told you about stopping Bill. I don't care how you do it, but stop him. You know what I mean."

Tess's small voice was barely audible. "I'll try."

"Damn it!" Tabor struggled violently, desperately, trying to get back to her, but the two beef-heavy cops almost yanked the wind out of him going out into the hall. Sweat was pouring from his hair, cascading down his face. Some got into his eyes and stung them. Then he shouted at Tess's closed door. "You better do more than try, damn it! You better make sure you stop him."

Less Beef jerked him again, toward the self-service elevator. "You wanna butt your head against a blackjack, boy?"

"Go to hell!" Tabor glared at him, breathing hard. He turned to the other cop. "What am I supposed to have beaten those clowns for?"

"Ten thousand simoleons and a couple of suitcases with some suits and jewelry in 'em."

They got on the elevator and Less Beef, still looking like he wanted to burn somebody, closed the steel door and punched a button that dropped them toward the main floor. For the first time since he'd left his hotel this afternoon, Tabor's belly let him know it hadn't been greased lately by growling three times. Then he thought of Bill, of what was likely to happen to him if Tess couldn't get him off the Andrews deal, and lost all taste for food. The elevator came to a smooth stop.

As they squeezed out of the elevator, three abreast, Tabor questioned Big Beef again. "Where're the suitcases?" He knew they had the answer to that too. Any frame that Arky Calahan concocted would be vice-tight.

"According to the complaining witnesses," the cop explained, "you didn't come directly here. You first went to a hotel on West Wells Street. You left the suitcases there, so they told the captain. You live on West Wells?"

The frame was complete. The two pieces of luggage would be waiting in his apartment.

"Mind if we take a look at your place before we make the station, or do we have to get a warrant?"

He minded. But he knew they'd get a search warrant and come back by themselves. They made his hotel in thirty minutes. At the door to his room, Tabor suddenly put on brakes. Inside, the lights were on, his record player was giving out soft music, and a pair of pink panties were draped over the arm of a plush-cushioned chair.

"What's the score, Tabor?"

"Somebody's in there, Lieutenant. And nobody's supposed to be."

"Well, let's take a peep," Less Beef said. He hauled out his .38 Colt automatic and snicked the safety off.

They went in. The sound of the door closing drew a strange, inquiring feminine voice through the open doorway of his kitchen. "Tank? That you, sweetheart? In the kitchen, dear. I'm making medicine. Come on, let's get knocked out together, then lay up and send each other."

There was only the sound of the soft music coming from the record player across the room in the apartment when the strange feminine voice stopped speaking. Tabor realized the cops were looking at him. With them hitching a ride on his heels, he led the way across the thickly carpeted sitting room to the kitchen door.

Less Beef gave out with a soft dirty-minded chuckle. "So nobody's supposed to be here, eh, boy?"

Tabor kept quiet, feeling trapped, also like a damn fool.

She was sitting in the breakfast nook, a blonde kid no older than sixteen or seventeen, and the only thing she was clothed in was the soft light from the florescent lamp on the wall opposite her. She didn't look up. They stood in the doorway gaping at her. Her left arm, wrapped tightly above the elbow with a brown calfskin belt Tabor recognized as his own, was outstretched on the table. She was absorbed in the job of shooting junk into a vein in the bend of the arm, using an eyedropper syringe. Scattered on the table were several empty capsules, a gold cigarette lighter and a tablespoon with a fire-blackened bowl.

Tabor didn't look at the cops. He wanted to run, wanted to chance breaking through the screened window on the other side of the kitchen and escaping down the fire escape. But he stood glued in the doorway, watching Calahan's frame tightening around him.

Without looking up, the little chippie loosened the belt on her arm with her teeth and let the junk flow through her bloodstream. Then, still without glancing their way, she closed her eyes and sucked in a long breath like she'd just come out of a fifteen-minute clinch with Porfirio Rubirosa. Her voice, when she spoke, was a bedroom moan. "Oh, Tank, baby. This last shot you gave me is a *wig*."

He started for her, took two steps, and the cops grabbed his arms and snatched him back. The chippie looked up then. She let out a little yelp. She took the spike out of her vein and sat there looking stupidly at Tabor, wet mouth slack, eyes blinking foolishly.

"How old are you, kid?" Less Beef asked.

"Sixteen." Her gaze swung from Tabor to the cops. Shiny tears began spilling down pinched cheeks. "He made me do it! I never wanted to start using stuff, but he made me."

Tabor stared at her, his face stony. There was no sense in wasting time trying to get her to go honest. Although she was young, she was a hardened little bitch. A beginner wouldn't have been able to give the five-star performance she was coming on with.

Less Beef indicated Tabor with his automatic. "Who? Him?"

She sniffled and did a bad job of hiding her nakedness with her hands. The junk had hit her and she was nodding and scratching and trying to keep her eyelids open. "Ye—yes, sir. He started me out on stuff. I didn't want to do it. Honest, officer."

"You son-of-a-bitch," Less Beef snarled, and came up with the flat side of his automatic.

Handcuffed as Tabor was, there was no getting out of the way. The heavy automatic caught him on the point of his chin, spun him completely around and sent him to his knees, dazed and hurt. His head felt like a million firecrackers were popping off in it. Somebody was saying something but the ringing in his ears made the words a jumble of nothing. He knelt there swaying and shaking his head, wishing the room would stop doing the loop the loop. After a while it did. He shoved himself to his feet and turned to look at the bastard cop who had slugged him. He tried to get his knees to stop wobbling so he could set himself and go up the side of the bastard's head with his handcuffed wrists. Then he changed his mind. The automatic in the cop's fist was even with his belly button.

"Lay off, Jacoby," the Lieutenant cut in. He looked at the girl. "How long have you been here?"

"Three days." A whining note had come into her voice.

She was nodding and blinking her heavy-lidded eyes all over the kitchen, at everyone but Tabor. "Tank wouldn't leave me go."

The big lieutenant looked at her a long time but his hard face showed nothing of what he was thinking. He said finally; "Did Tabor come by here tonight and leave two suitcases?"

The girl jerked her head up and down quickly, as if eager to answer, never once meeting Tabor's eyes. "Yes, sir. Two large brown ones. They're in our bedroom."

"What're you getting out of this?" Tabor asked quietly.

All he got for an answer was silence.

The Lieutenant said, "Okay, girlie. Get some clothes on. The captain will wanna talk to you."

Chapter Six

The cell was lightless and a size smaller than a fifty-cent flophouse bedroom. It smelled strongly of disinfectant. Tabor prowled the few feet of space between the front bars and the foul-smelling toilet bowl on the back wall. He'd been mugged, fingerprinted, relieved of everything he had in his pockets but his handkerchief and cigarettes, and booked on one count of forcing a minor to use dope, on two counts of armed robbery and on still another of assault with intent to kill.

There was another guy in the cell with him, Jock Adams, a soft-talking young Negro with a lot of humor in his alert eyes, and about a hundred and twenty-five greenies worth of neatly cut Palm Beach suit on his giant frame. Jock's ex-spouse had had him tossed in the slammer, claiming he was two thousand dollars behind in his alimony. According to Jock though, her story wasn't pure. He claimed it was a pressure job to get him to see things her way. It seemed that she'd run down on him over in Chicago a few weeks ago in the downtown nightclub where he was tending bar and tried to sweet talk him into kissing and making up, but he'd decided he'd had enough of a gal who woke up mornings with her fists balled and smiled only when she was in some nightclub deflating their bank account.

"Know something, Tank?" he said.

"What's that?"

Jock was stretched out on the top bunk, a scarred piece of naked steel, with his hands locked behind his head and his feet propped up on the back wall. "The little chippie that helped Arky Calahan set you up for this bust—she sounds familiar to me. Say her name's Ramona Harris?"

"That's the one she gave the cops."

"Yellow-colored hair, shapely stems? A nice face that used to be pretty, only now it's thin from shooting too much stuff?"

Tabor squeezed around at the front of the cell and leaned back against the bars. "I don't know what her face's thin from, but that's the babe."

"Thought so," Jock said, nodding his head. "That chippie's been sending eight and nine guys a year to the joint for Arky for the last three years. Petty dope pushers that got in Arky's way. Guys he didn't want to bother killing. Only before this deal of yours she always set the fellows up for carnal-knowledge-and-abuse raps. She's Florence and Booker Harris' kid. They got a ten-year jolt for stuff and white slavery a few years back. Goaldie. That's the name she sports around the corners."

"Who does Goaldie live with now?"

"A jive mackman named Albino had her when I was here before. Matter of fact, he turned her out when she first jumped out on the track, four years ago. You should know Albino. He's another Arky Calahan flunkie."

There was a question on Tabor's lips, but the wino in the next cell began raising hell again. Off and on, for the past half hour, he'd been banging his tin cup on the bars and yelling if somebody didn't bring him a pint of muscatel to cool his fever he'd drink out of the toilet-house bowl. Only he didn't say toilet-house.

The wino finally let up on the banging and yelling and Tabor got his question to Jock. "How do you know so much about Calahan and his clowns?"

"Used to pick up numbers for him a few years back."

"Why'd you stop?"

The big guy was quiet for a moment, knuckling his chin thoughtfully. "When I first started working for Arky, I thought I was the hungriest guy in the world, but shortly afterward I decided I wasn't that hungry. Anyway, not hungry enough to work for a bastard who'd have his thugs make junkies out of his sister's kids—two teen-age girls—just because she wouldn't let him stash dope on her property. That's Arky."

The big steel door up front squeaked open and the turnkey, a jelly-bellied pipe smoker, clumped down the narrow hall that ran along the front of the cells. He stopped in front of their cell. A switch clicked and a yellowed bulb over the keeper's hairless head gave out a stingy blob of light. Tabor saw he had a package in his hand. It smelled good. Like food.

Tank asked, "Can I call my lawyer now, pop?"

"Son, I told you to see your arresting officers."

"Those bastards—" He started to beef and thought better of it. The guy was only obeying orders. "Okay, pop. What you got there? I'm hungry."

The old man slid the package through the food slot in the bars. "For Jock Adams. A Vivian Quantrel's out front, but the sarge won't let her visit with you. She asked do you need any money."

"Tell her I don't need anything but out." The big colored guy turned over on his side and raised himself up on his forearm. "Also tell her I say be down here as soon as the doors open tomorrow morning and take care of the business."

"Yeah, yeah, lover boy." The turnkey sucked wetly at his pipe, got it to fouling up the air some more with acrid smoke, then said: "I'll leave the light on so's you can see your chow." He scuffled back up the narrow hail, asking the wino next door had he emptied the toilet bowl yet.

Tabor held the package out to Jock. "Here. Smells good."

"Go on, knock yourself out, man." Jock turned over on his back again. "I just downed a steak dinner a little while before you came in."

"Thanks."

He sat down on the bottom bunk and unwrapped the package. It was a fried chicken dinner and still warm. He ate slowly, not tasting the food, though, just thinking about his brother.

"Just think," Jock said, breaking the deep silence that had settled over the jail, "if I'd been able to spy on Arky, like the Feds wanted me to, all this grief probably wouldn't be coming your way now."

"The Feds wanted you to spy on Calahan?"

"Yeah. About six months back some news reporter got himself wasted and they figured Arky and his boys had a lot to do with it—no proof, though. Wanted to plant a mike on me and have me walk around Arky's boys when they got to yakking. They said a mobile unit would've been parked close by to pick up on every word of their talks. There wouldna been too much for me to worry about, only I'd torn it too bad with Arky and when I hit on him about picking up numbers again, he said he wouldn't even let me pick up his cigar butts." Jock chuckled. "It seems that Mr. Calahan doesn't go for anybody blowing him out and walking off his job. You remember that reporter's killing, don't you?"

Tabor remembered it well. For weeks after it had happened the newspaper reporter's murder had been front-page news. The reporter had been a racket-buster and made statements in public that he was about ready to squash the racketeers and crooked politicians in Milwaukee. Only before the guy had been able to reveal the lethal evidence he was supposed to have had, he'd come up dead, blasted apart in his car by a double charge from a sawed-off shotgun. The killer or killers were still on the loose.

Tank swallowed a piece of chicken, then said: "I remember the case, but what brought the Feds in on it? The guy wasn't government property."

"No, but he got it a few feet across the Wisconsin-Illinois state line, on the Illinois side. That gave the F.B.I. jurisdiction. Sure wish I could've helped 'em grab Arky, though. That bastard wanna make junkies out of every college and high school kid in the city."

Gabbing about something besides his own troubles was easing the pressure off Tabor's nerves a little. The food was helping some, too. "Think Arky had a hand in having the guy bumped?" he asked Jock.

"I dunno," he said. "Some Illinois law was over here questioning him about it, but apparently they didn't get anything." Jock shifted on his bunk, then was quiet a moment. "You can do your own adding, though, Tank. The reporter let it be known he was out to bust the racket boys and tainted politicians, and Arky's Mr. Big around this town. Take it from there."

"It adds."

The chicken dinner finished, Tabor stretched out on his back on the bunk. The cool steel didn't give an inch. Up on the top bunk Jock moved around, restless. Tabor saw the shadow of the big guy's arm high up on the wall, heard his lighter click, then smelled cigarette smoke.

Jock rolled on his stomach and looked over the side of the think?" at him, his brown face serious, "Know what I think?"

"No. What?"

"I don't think you're going to get to make a phone call, or see anybody, either. That turnkey was supposed to let you contact your lawyer. I think those cops put an N. C. O. tag on you. It's not legal, but I'd bet my choice babe against a three-dollar bill that that's what's going on."

"N. C. O.?"

"Yeah. No communication outside." Jock reached through the bars, tapped the ash off his cigarette onto the hall floor. "If everything you say about Calahan and your brother's true, you can bet the cops are going to have the judge put your bail out of reach of your bankroll when you go to court in the morning, too."

Tabor turned over to let the steel bunk hurt his left side a while. "Think the judge'll listen to them?"

"He'll listen. More than likely he'll be Calahan's

man."

Jock hauled at his cigarette, blew smoke toward the wall. "Tank, I'm gonna give it to you like it is—if you don't execute some damn good gimmicks soon you won't hit the bricks again for the next twenty years. Forcing a minor to use coke is good for a thirty-five-year jolt and those two armed robbery beefs and that assault rap'll swell the thirty-five to a hundred and ten years. You can forget about that you're-innocent-until-proven-guilty crap. When these bastards get somebody to rap you you're guilty as hell in their book until *you* prove otherwise. And, fellow, you gotta have a lot of proof to satisfy these people."

The same thoughts had been banging around inside Tabor's head. But hearing someone voice them made them seem more for real, not so fantastic. He broke out in a sweat. With every second that galloped by the cell seemed to get tighter, the foul air harder to breathe. Every goddamn thing was wrong.

He had to get out of there.

He got up and did what the wine addict in the next cell had been doing, yelling and banging his tin cup on the bars. "Turnkey! Turnkey!"

The wise eyes of Jock watched him, but the big guy said nothing, just watched understandingly, giving the right side of his thick neck a slow rub with his right hand.

Tabor banged the bars harder with the cup, hollered louder. "Turnkey!" He listened for the squeak of the steel door up front, feeling the sweat soaking his undershirt.

During the quiet the wino next door gave out with a harsh cackle and called over to him. "Hey, buddy. You got 'em too, eh? The joker might slip us a bottle if we both tell him we're gonna drink outa the—"

Up front the steel door slammed, drowning out the

wino's voice. The pot-gutted jailer started to stop at the wino's but Tabor told him he was the one who had called. The turnkey's gray eyebrows were jammed together and his old eyes were smoldering. That was all right. He was hot too. Hot and scared.

"Look," Tank said, before the old guy could blow him out. "I *have* to make a phone call. I can't wait for those cops to get big-hearted. A life depends on it."

The wind left the turnkey's jelly-belly in one long tired sigh. "At least you could tell me a fresh joke, son, after all the hell you raised to get me back here. You been around, I hear. Don't you know no meaty whorehouse jokes?"

The old guy wasn't making him happy as hell to know him. "I'm not making funny, pop," he said, his voice tense.

"Son, I been conned by the best."

"Look. You can listen in while I talk. Just let me make one call."

The turnkey came on with the slow headshake again. "Ain't nothing I can do till your arresting officers say so."

Jock asked him, "What about me? Can I make one?"

"You already went the limit, lover."

Tabor gripped one of the bars so tightly his fingers burned. Then he relaxed. The turnkey had turned away, snapped off the light, and was clumping back up the narrow hall.

"I'll be able to take a message out for you in the morning," Jock told him.

Tabor tossed the tin cup back into the sink and got back on the slab of merciless steel. "Think you'll beat your rap?" The quarter was mechanical. His eyes were open, staring upward at the bottom of Jock's bunk. But all he could see was Bill trying desperately to keep a jump ahead of Calahan and his gunsels.

Droplets of sweat rolled from the edges of his hair onto his neck.

Jock's soft chuckle brought his mind back. "There won't be a rap on me in the morning. I'd put up my choice babe against a nickel bag of peanuts on that. The food was   ex-old lady's way of letting me know all is forgiven."

"Hope you're right," Tabor said. "If you cut out in the morning maybe you can do me some good."

At ten o'clock the next morning Tank was trying to wear out the dirty concrete floor of the cell. He'd been to court. The judge, apparently one of Calahan's, had given him a week to get ready for his arraignment and slapped a fifty-grand bail on him. The high bail wasn't the cause of his zoo parade. Six grand to a bondsman would street him. The turnkey was the cause of the calisthenics.

He growled, "What the hell's happened to that turnkey? He's had an hour to get a bondsman over here."

Jock thumped his cigarette butt in the general direction of the toilet bowl, and said quietly: "You won't get a bondsman, Tank."

Tabor jerked to a stop. His head came up sharply. "You clowning on me?"

But even as he asked he knew the big guy wasn't goofing. His cocoa-brown face wasn't wearing its usual smile. It was sober.

"No," Jock said, returning his stare. He slow-rubbed the side of his neck. "No, I'm giving it to you like I know it is. We don't have but two bondsmen in the city and every time they hear Arky Calahan's name they turn to the east and salaam for twenty minutes. Didn't think of this last night. Nothing but fifty grand cash or a hundred grand in property will pull you outa here."

Tabor felt like he'd bailed out of a plane at five miles, up and suddenly realized he didn't have on a parachute.

He fumbled a cigarette and a match out of his jacket pocket. After six or seven unsuccessful tries at striking the match on his thumbnail, he cursed softly and flung it through the bars into the hall. It hit the wall and broke into flame. He took a light off the silver cigarette lighter Jock held out to him. Then he went back on the prowl and began a mental count of his dough. He could forget about six grand of it, the amount he'd had on him when he got busted. The cops had confiscated that as part of the money Trigger Slim and Moe claimed he'd taken from them in that phony holdup beef.

So that left the twenty or twenty-five G's he had in the bank and the nine or ten grand stashed in his apartment. That was all the loot he had and the money in the bank was dead to him, because it was a four-star fact that the cops weren't going to let him go and sign it out, and that was the only way he could get it.

He paused, squinting his eyes and pulling absently at his cigarette. There were two people who'd street him. His gal Kate and Steve Novack. Steve was no longer a racket boss. He was now a saloon owner. Steve owed him a couple of favors, and he and Kate had, or could get, the kind of money he needed to get out on bail. He looked at Jock.

"If you quit the scene this morning, I want you to do a thing or two for me."

"Name 'em."

"I've got about ten grand in my apartment. Get it, then call Kate Lamain and tell her to make up the balance of my bail. If she doesn't have the whole forty grand, take her over to Steve Novack's joint and have her get what she's short of from him. Steve knows Kate. He'll give her the dough."

"This the Steve Novack the cops pulled in for questioning when that newspaper reporter got bumped?"

"I didn't know Steve was hauled in for that."

"May not be the same guy," Jock said, crossing his long legs. "This guy was an old gangster the cops claim knows more about what's going on in the rackets today than most of the active hoods. They didn't figure he'd bumped the reporter but thought maybe they could get him to steer them in the direction of the guys who did. The old guy didn't tell them what the bird left on the fence."

Tabor nodded. "That's Steve. Will you do that for me?"

The big colored guy's eyes narrowed with incredulity. He looked at Tabor a long time, still thoughtfully massaging the side of his neck.

"You'd trust me with your ten grand? You don't even know me."

"I don't have much of a choice. It's either I trust you to come through or sit here like a nut and wait for Arky Calahan to murder my brother and lose me in the penitentiary. I'll place my bets on you."

He heard the front door being opened, then the day turnkey's hard heels clicking on the cement floor. Without waiting for Jock to make any comment he gave him the address of his hotel and told him where he had the ten G's stashed.

The smile came back on Jock's face, only broader now, revealing glistening white teeth. "This is something new. Somebody trusting me. You know something, man?"

"What's that?"

"I kinda like the feeling of being trusted. Even

though it's a forced issue." He stuck out his ham-sized hand and Tabor gripped it. The big guy didn't have a hand, he had a vice. They finished trying to crush each other's bones to a fine powder and Jock said: "You picked yourself a winner, man. I don't understand it, but I'll be damned if you didn't."

The day man stopped before their cell. It was on his sweaty red face, the bad news, and Tabor knew Jock had been right about the bondsmen and Calahan.

The turnkey spread his hands, palms up. "No bondsman for you, Tabor. They say you're a bad risk." He looked at Jock. "Going out, Adams. The charge against you was dropped."

Tabor moved away from the door so Jock could hop down from the bunk.

"I'll take care of the business," Jock said, fastening his shirt collar. He slapped a twenty-greenie Leghorn on his head, then asked: "But how do I get in?"

Tabor looked at the turnkey. "Can he get a key out of my personal belongings?"

"Sure."

He told Jock which key it was and then watched the turnkey let the big guy out, feeling glad to see him go. But when the cell door clanked shut again and the big bolt clicked into place, he winced.

He said to Jock: "Call up Tess Andrews and ask her about my brother, won't you?"

"That's the first thing," Jock said, and waved so long.

After their footsteps died and the outside door squeaked open and banged shut, he sat down on the side of his bunk and stared at the shadows of the bars on the bleak gray walls of the cell. Tendrils of smoke drifted past his eyes from the cigarette stub in the corner of his mouth. He thought of Kate, of how good she'd always been to him. He'd give anything to be able to feel about her the way he felt about Tess.

Tess. Even thinking of her and her fineness excited him.

Come out of it, boy. Come out of it. You can't do anything there but foul out. Tess isn't throwing anything but bad pitches, he told himself. He took a long pull off the butt and drowned it in the toilet bowl, wondering if he'd ever be able to come out from under Tess's spell.

Then yawning tiredly, he stretched out on the steel torture rack, pillowing his head with his arm.

Chapter Seven

Tabor was released on a fifty-thousand-dollar cash bail at six-fifty that afternoon. His personal belongings were given back to him, everything but a neat six G's. They told him they had picked up his car and he would find it at the police parking lot across from the street from the jail. The big lobby was crammed with off-duty cops and cops just coming on. More than a few of them stopped yakking and stared at him with surprise as he weaved through them and pushed around the tall revolving doors out onto the sidewalk. Before long he knew Calahan and his clowns would have the news of his release.

He wondered what they'd try to do then.

Pausing on the long concrete steps of the jailhouse, Tabor searched along the curbs, looking for Kate and Jock. He didn't see either of them. That was odd—one of them should have waited around for him.

He glanced at his watch again. It was seven straight up. Still no Kate or Jock. Breathing deeply of the clean air, he left the steps of the jail and went to the police parking lot and recovered the Caddy.

About two blocks from the parking lot, Tabor,

glancing in the rearview mirror, noticed a green Chrysler three or four cars back cutting recklessly in and out of the heavy traffic. The car looked familiar, but was too far back for him to identify the driver. At the next corner he left Wells Street and pulled over to the curb on the cross street. The green Sedan whipped around the corner and came to a rocking stop behind him.

Kate Lamain was in the car.

Tabor got out and met her. She ran to him, calling his name in a choked but happy voice. She flung herself against him and threw her arms around his waist.

He was too worried to appreciate the feel of her soft body against his. "Where's Jock?" he asked.

"Jock?"

"Yeah. The big colored guy who told you about the bail."

Kate let go of his waist and pushed her hair back with her hands. "No colored guy named Jock told me about you," she said, shaking her head slowly. "I called your hotel this morning to ask how you had come out with Bill and the desk clerk told me about you leaving with two detectives and a girl last night. Was he supposed to call my place?"

He nodded. "Yeah. This morning."

"What time?"

"Sometime after ten-thirty."

"Then he might've tried to call me," she said. "I've been in the city since nine this morning. I had a heck of a time trying to get some information about you. Finally I ran across Mike. You know, the patrolman who used to come out to the house when we were together? I got him to give out with what you were being held for and the amount of your bail."

He squeezed her shoulders affectionately. "Thanks,

doll. Heard anything about Bill?"

"No one has seen him. I called his home but he wasn't in. His wife said he left for the District Attorney's office early this morning." Those tiny pain wrinkles appeared at the corners of Kate's eyes. Her voice was troubled.

"Tank, he hasn't been in to see the District Attorney. I just came from asking about him in the District Attorney's office. They're waiting for him, and, Tank, they're worried. The District Attorney kept asking did I have any idea where he is. Asked me that four times in the few minutes I was in his office."

They stood a moment, looking at each other, neither of them saying anything. He didn't like this news. Bill always kept his appointments. "Until this thing's over maybe you'd better go over to Chicago and stay," he said. "Calahan won't like your crossing him. He didn't intend for me to get out on bail. Keep in touch, though."

Kate shook her head. "I'll be all right here. But what about you? You'll have to do something about those phony charges on you or they'll railroad you to prison, Tank."

"I know. Soon as I get Bill straight, I'll start working on those."

"Need any money?"

"Uh-uh, baby. Thanks, anyway. Go home now. I'll call you later."

Kate pulled his head down, kissed him softly on his mouth. She tried to grin after that but it didn't come off.

Abruptly she turned away and ran to her car. He watched her drive off and then got into the Caddy and headed for his hotel. He needed a gun.

Chapter Eight

With the exception of The Strip, a small bar next to his hotel, all of the nightclubs in the block were lit up. Tabor squeezed into a slot at the curb in front of his hotel and cut off the engine. As he got out of the car a light gray sedan cruised slowly by. The driver had his head turned the other way. He watched the gray car until it made a right turn at the corner. He had the feeling that the driver had been big-eyeing him. He shrugged it off.

A wave of cool sweet-smelling air caressed his face as he stepped into the expensive lobby of his hotel. Several high-powered hookers with a lot of creamy mound-shaped meat bulging over the tops of daringly low-cut dresses were giving some of the plush chairs a feel of their choice parts. Lucky chairs, he thought. The babes took in his bum-like appearance with raised eyebrows. He grunted. The fakes. As if anything could shock them. The cute red-headed clerk was her same sweet self. As always whenever he came in, she smiled and invited him to her bedroom with her eyes. He winked back, but his heart wasn't in it.

He walked up the short flight of thickly carpeted stairs, turned down the long hall toward his apartment. The hall was quiet, the numbered doors on either side of it, closed. He hoped Bill was all right. The kid had a family to live for. And if he wasn't all right, Tabor knew he'd kill Calahan.

He let himself into his apartment, pulled the chain on the floor lamp beside a deep chair, and headed for his bedroom. He wanted to see if Jock had beaten him for his poke. It was hard for him to believe the big guy had double-crossed him.

At that moment someone out front jumped up and down on a car horn three times. Then he heard another sound that shocked him to a sudden stop. Four loud blasts from a heavy-calibered revolver beat off the walls of the apartment, echoing and re-echoing like rumbles of thunder.

The shots came from his kitchen.

With fear plucking at his nerves like a bass player's fingers plucking at the strings of a fiddle, he grabbed up two heavy brass book ends from an end table and ran toward the kitchen. The deep-napped rug on the floor deadened the sound of his reckless approach. As he came to the kitchen door he saw somebody climb out his window and disappear down the fire escape. He ran to the window and looked out.

The man who had run down the fire escape was diving into the back seat of the light gray sedan he had seen cruising by out front a few minutes ago. The car moved off, going slowly, apparently so as not to attract any attention and disappeared around the corner.

Tabor didn't have to do much figuring to know who the guy was. That oily black hair and the big body and pink sports jacket he'd seen belonged to Monkey Face Moe. The gore freak.

Setting the heavy book ends on the breakfast nook seat, he turned away from the window and saw what the gunsel had been cutting loose at.

It was as if someone had grabbed his heart valves and was steadily applying pressure to them.

Bill sat propped in a corner, his head hanging forward loosely. Blood was gushing out of the front of his neck, running down his shirt.

Almost falling in his haste, Tabor ran to the corner and knelt beside him. He lifted his brother's chin gently. Bill was still alive. The bullet wounds were nasty and his breath was rattling in his throat, but maybe there was still a chance for the kid. There had to be.

He slid one arm under Bill's thighs, the other around his back. The kid had to have a doctor in a hurry. Taking him to one himself was the fastest way he could think of. The hospital was just a few blocks west. Slowly he started to lift up with Bill, fighting down the sickness in his stomach that was trying to break out.

Pain twisted Bill's clean features. His glazed eyes tried to focus themselves. "No," he rasped as Tabor straightened up with him. "Please! No."

"Easy does it, boy," Tabor said softly. "Easy does it."

The sound of his voice got through to Bill. His eyes cleared. He pulled weakly at his sleeve. "Tank, no. I-I'm going. Tess tried to s-stop me, Ta—" He coughed and flecks of blood came out of the corners of his mouth. "D-don't blame her. P-promise, Tank."

Swallowing hard, Tabor nodded at him. "I promise. Don't talk anymore."

He carried Bill out of the kitchen, making for the front door. He wanted to run but he took it as easy as he could. They were almost across the living room when Bill coughed again and let out a long rustling breath. The hand on his sleeve fell and swung without control.

Tabor's face was so stiff the muscles along his temples ached. Slowly he turned and laid Bill's body on the studio couch. For a few seconds he stood there looking down at him, feeling the pressure building up in him. The kid hadn't even got his heater out. It was still in his shoulder holster. He took the snub-nose .38 and stuck it into his hip pocket.

He'd need it.

Turning, he went into his bedroom. The bed had

been made up, but a faint scent of the dime-store perfume the little chippie Goaldie used was still in the air. He'd have to find that little lying junkie bitch.

A glance inside his clothes closet told him his loot was gone. The green tin box he'd kept the bread in was on the floor. Open and empty. He took a brown lightweight suit, a sports shirt and a pair of shoes from the closet. From the top shelf he took down his .357 Magnum and a box of ammunition. This was the first time he'd had the gun down in almost a year. He knew how to use it. A guy who made his living gambling with the racket boys had to have a fast gun hand or he'd get wasted in a hurry for winning so often.

As he checked the gun he became aware of the faint baying of a siren rising and falling, drawing nearer.

His mind latched on to a nasty suspicion and wouldn't let it go.

He ran to the front door. It wasn't necessary to open the door. The excited chatter of his fast-life neighbors coming in through the open transom was plenty plain. They were wondering where the gunshots had come from. He was wondering about the open transom. He'd always kept it closed.

Stuffing the gun and ammunition in his pockets, he struck a trot back to the kitchen. When he looked out the kitchen window he looked down into the upturned faces of a curious crowd.

He got away from the window fast, his breath harsh in his throat. The picture was clear now, his suspicion confirmed. He'd been had—been set up again—this time to take the rap for his brother's murder.

For a second he thought of trying to get Bill's body out of the apartment but remembered his neighbors out in the corridor. The only thing he could do was get himself out. If he got caught now he'd spend the rest of his life staring at the shadows of the bars on the bleak gray walls of a prison cell. Nobody would believe he was clean, that he hadn't killed Bill, not with all the other charges he had hanging over him.

He hastily gathered up the clothes he'd laid out in his bedroom, got the clip holster for the Magnum from the dresser drawer and then went through Bill's clothes. It was hard, feeling the kid's lifeless body, looking at the frozen expression of agony on his face. There was nothing in Bill's pockets but a wallet and a couple of handkerchiefs. The wallet went into the jacket pocket of the suit he was taking with him. Bill's wife and kids needed the few dollars in it more than the cops did.

The corridor was alive with people. All talk did a slow fade as they noted Tabor's appearance.

He couldn't have looked inconspicuous if he'd tried, not as grimy as he was and with his pockets bagging with a pair of heaters, a box of ammunition, and an assortment of other stuff. He didn't try. Without pausing he nodded at several fine young things he'd shacked up with a few times. They didn't nod back, just stared wide-eyed, with their red ripe lips hanging open with surprise and curiosity.

He tried not to walk too fast but it was hard as hell not to. The baying of what he knew was a police siren, sounded close, too close, almost like it was in the basement of the hotel.

At the curb he threw the clothes on the back seat of the Caddy. Then he felt the fine hairs on the back of his neck stand up, as a squad car cut diagonally in front of his car and braked to a quick stop.

A plain-clothes cop was jumping out before the squad had ceased rocking. "Hold it, Tabor," he yelled.

And he was grabbing under his coat for his heater.

Chapter Nine

He didn't hold it. Wheeling away from the Caddy, he ran back the way the squad car had come. Behind him the cop was yelling, telling him to halt or he'd shoot. The skin on his back quivered but he didn't even think about obeying the cop.

He bent lower, grunted harder, and ran like hell, holding his suit coat pockets to keep the Magnum and the box of ammunition from banging against his thighs. He stumbled, went to one knee. The shock sped all the way up to his stomach. Cursing softly and breathing hard, he glanced back over his shoulder. The detective was about fifty yards back and was cutting down that distance fast with a ground-eating sprint. His heater was in his fist now.

Scrambling to his feet, Tabor ran hard for neon lights a couple of buildings away. He whipped into the bar and kept on toward the rear door. Some of the thirsters at the bar knocked over their stools getting to their feet. He saw the startled expression on the barman's face, saw him duck down behind the bar; then he was slamming into the back screen door and stumbling out into the alley.

He didn't linger there. He hot-footed to the corner, wheezed over to Wells Street again, and almost yanked the door off getting into a cab that had just discharged a diamond-studded fly-guy and a giggling brunette.

"Get going," Tabor panted at the cabbie. "Fast."

The cabbie had a nasty word on his lips and an angry glint in his eyes. But after a closer look at Tabor's face he changed his mind. Glancing through the cab's rear window, Tabor saw the cop hadn't shown on the scene.

When he turned back around the cabbie asked, "Where to, buddy?" in a shaky voice with half of his eyes on the rearview mirror, watching him.

After he had gulped his breath back to normal he told the cabbie where to take him.

"Dame trouble?" the cabbie probed.

Tabor gave him no answer and he took the hint and just drove. Tabor mopped the sweat off his face and neck, then dug out a cigarette, lit it, and stared out the window.

There was an awful sickness inside him. Although, during the past several years, he and Bill had strayed farther away from each other, his feeling for Bill had never changed. Now Bill was gone, and all he had left were the memories. A feeling of bitter loneliness came over him.

Frowning distastefully, he thumped his half-smoked cigarette through the window. Nearly two days had passed since he'd brushed his teeth and the hunk of baloney he'd eaten while in the slammer had his mouth sour. But he soon forgot about the sour taste in his mouth and thought of the fix he was in.

Calahan would see to it that the cops would find evidence of his guilt some place in his apartment, just as they'd found the two suitcases he was supposed to have got off Trigger Slim and Moe in a heist. But this latest frame was neater than the others Calahan had wrapped around him. With this one Calahan would have the help of a flock of witnesses, strong witnesses, people who were not in his organization, people who'd stand up under any kind of cross-examination, because they'd be telling the truth about what they'd heard and seen.

That wouldn't prove that he'd killed Bill. But it showed he hadn't followed his usual happy-neighbor routine. With a jury that would mean something. The prosecutor would paint an ugly picture for the jury with his questions and interpretations of the testimony of the witnesses; Bill's body in his apartment; and the fact he'd left it in such a hurry.

Yeah, he thought, a jury would convict him. He couldn't prove he hadn't murdered his brother.

The frame had been worked perfectly, too. Monkey Face Moe and the driver of the light gray sedan had let him get into his apartment, then made damn sure he couldn't get out again without being seen. The four gunshots had taken care of that. Those shots had called his place to the attention of every swinging fanny in the vicinity.

Arky Calahan had viced the hell out of him, he thought grimly, knuckling his chin tiredly.

Then another fact rocked home and made him sweat some more.

If he went through with what he had in mind, doing in Calahan and Moe, he'd be on the run for the rest of his life. That would be playing a losing game. He couldn't run and hide forever, the police would catch up with him, and he knew he would die then. Letting them grab him and send him up for life was out of the question. A lifetime is hard enough to live in the free world, he thought, let alone in the penitentiary.

There was only one clean out for him: Make Ritchie Andrews' and Bill's murders boomerang on Arky Calahan.

Tabor leaned forward and tapped the cabbie on the shoulder. "I've changed my mind about that address," he told him, then gave him Tess's address. He had to pick up where Bill had left off.

Frowning faintly, Tabor glanced at his watch. Eight-thirty. The sour baloney taste was still in his mouth and a nasty thought that was beginning to slither through his mind was worsening the condition. How had Calahan been able to time his last frame so perfectly? Had Kate set him up for Calahan?

Something inside him twisted up. No. He. couldn't go for that. Not Kate. Anyone else maybe, but not her.

Sometime later he heard the cabbie's voice saying, "Hey, buddy. Your number. We've arrived."

Tabor came back to this world and saw they were parked in front of Tess's canopied entrance. He went to his pants pocket for the cab fare. Then he realized he didn't have a nickel of any kind of money. Bill's wallet was in the suit he'd run off and left. Hell, he'd even forgotten to get his bank book. He cursed Jock for beating him for his poke.

"Wait here," Tabor said to the cabbie. "Be right back."

With the gun and the box of ammunition in his coat pockets bumping his thighs, Tabor went into the clean vestibule, punched Tess's bell.

A vaguely familiar man's voice asked, "Who's there?"

"Tell Tess it's Tank." He became aware of a frown on his face. Then he got hot at himself for getting pepped up about a guy being up in Tess's apartment.

The door buzzed and he went up in the self-service elevator, but not until he'd fed the Magnum. The guy upstairs didn't have to be Tess's friend.

Jock, his twenty-dollar Leghorn in his hand, stood in the doorway of Tess's apartment, grinning at him. "Man, you look whipped." he observed.

There was no smile on Tabor's face for the soft-talking giant. He stood there in the hall, saying nothing, waiting for him to give out with his story.

The twinkle in Jock's eyes eased out, the brown face sobered. "What happened?" he asked, his voice even softer than usual.

"That's what I want you to tell me," Tabor answered, making no move to enter the apartment. "Where's my poke?"

"Here." Jock took a bundle of greenies from his pants pocket and gave it to Tabor.

The money was mostly hundreds and fifties. He thumbed through the bundle. It was all there. Close to twelve thousand. He pocketed the bundle. Then he looked up, opened him mouth to begin the question-and-answer routine, but clamped it tight again, as Tess came to stand in the doorway beside Jock.

"Tank!" she exclaimed, "What in the world happened to you?" She looked at him more closely. Big blue eyes got bigger. Soft red lips parted a little. There was dread in the words she spoke. "Bill's dead! I know it. He's been murdered!"

Tabor snapped, "Bawling won't bring him back. You should've stopped him before this happened."

"I tried, Tank," she sniffed. "Honestly I did."

"You didn't try hard enough." He felt anger pressing hard against his control. "You don't know what Bill had on Calahan?"

Tess moved her head from side to side, then got back on the same track she'd been on a moment ago. "I tried, Tank. I couldn't have done any more—please, Tank, don't look at me like that. I did everything I could to make him get off the case."

"Not everything. You could've used what you've always used to get what you wanted," Tabor said nastily, looking at her full ripe body. "But maybe Bill couldn't pay the price."

She moved in so fast he didn't have time to get back out of the way. The palm of her hand caught him a stinging blow on the mouth. "You filthy dog," she hissed, "Get out!"

Tabor started for her and Jock moved in front of him.

"Tank, you're wrong," he said softly, slowly. "Why don't you do some listening and find out what's happening first before you flip?"

Breathing harshly, Tabor looked at him. The guy was right. There was a lot here he didn't understand and going to war with Jock wouldn't help him get the answers.

Jock went on. "I found out a couple of things today."

"You got a short?" Tabor asked him, suddenly feeling the need to get moving. He knew it wouldn't be long before the cops got around to coming here looking for him.

"Downstairs," Jock said.

"Look. I need help. Only before you help me, I want you to know what you're doing." He looked at Tess. She had moved from behind Jock at the new note in his voice. Her big blue eyes were still wet with tears but no longer blazing with anger. "The cops want me bad," he said. "Calahan framed me with my brother's murder."

"Oh, no, Tank!" Tess cried, and came close and put her arms around his waist as if she would protect him from all harm. She said something else, but he was no longer tuned in on her.

Another sound had hit the air waves, a sound he was beginning to dread, the mournful wail of a siren. That one wasn't very far off, either, and drawing closer. "Let's get out of here, Jock."

Tess let go of him and stepped back. In her eyes was the same warm expression that Kate nearly always had in her eyes for him.

For a moment longer he looked at her tear-stained face, wanting her, feeling his manliness aching for her, and he tightened up on his control. Being chumped off once by her was enough for him.

Turning, he followed Jock down the stairs and left her standing there.

After Tabor straightened the scared cabbie he and

Jock got underway in Jock's new Roadmaster. The siren was still baying, and was no more than a couple of blocks away.

They had traveled five or six blocks in silence when Jock spoke up. "That girl you told me to contact about your bail—Kate Lamain. I called her place but nobody answered, and Steve Novack's out of town somewhere and won't be back till tomorrow night sometime. I figured Tess might have some idea where Kate might be so I called and told her what was happening with you and asked her if she knew where I could find her. She didn't. But you know what happened?"

"No," Tabor murmured, "What?"

"She said, 'I have thirty-five thousand dollars Tank can have.'"

Tabor looked around at Jock's smooth profile, trying to see if the guy was giving him a piece of fiction. He said, "Tess said that?"

Jock took a long pull at his cigarette, blew out smoke and words at the same time. "She said it and showed she meant it by getting every cent of it together. We came down to pull you out, but the desk sergeant told us somebody had bailed you already. Tess tried to get you at your hotel after we left the station, but the girl on the desk told her you'd come and gone, so we came to her place. Figuring you'd show there right away."

The baloney taste in Tabor's mouth was like quinine. He got rid of his cigarette, wiped the back of his hand across his lips. And he'd talked about her like a dog, when all the time she'd been in his corner, fighting for him, trying to help him save Bill. A skunk would have been justified in feeling clean and sweet beside him, he thought. The Roadmaster purred ahead smoothly. There'd been no mention of where they were going and he decided to leave that up to Jock. The big guy had been right all the way down the line so far.

"You forgot something," Tabor said.

"Did I?"

"Uh-huh. I was always pretty sharp at math. And no matter how hard I try, I can't get fifty grand out of Tess's thirty-five and my twelve."

"Oh, that," Jock said. "I scuffled up on the few more dollars we needed. It took a lot of lip work—that's why we got down to the station so late." He glanced at Tabor, "How tall are you?"

"Six-four."

"Around two hundred pounds?" Jock asked, and when Tabor nodded, he said, "My suits oughtta fit you pretty good."

From the start, Tabor had gone for Jock. Still, he couldn't help wondering why Jock had jumped all the way into his corner, especially since he'd worked for Calahan and knew the days ahead were going to be rugged as hell.

"How come?" he asked.

Jock shook his head, seeming to know what Tabor meant without him having told him. "I dunno," he said. "Maybe it's the way you made me feel when you trusted me with your geets. Nobody ever took me at face value before. Then maybe it's because Tess thinks you're worth helping. I was with her only a few hours, but that was long enough for me to find out she's a thoroughbred." He grinned and tossed his cigarette stub out the window. "Hell, man, I don't know—maybe I'm just a glutton for hard knocks."

"Helping me won't exactly get you on Calahan's honor roll."

The grin on Jock's face got bigger. "I don't think I was ever even close to making his honor roll, anyway." He made a right turn, and said, "I'm taking you to my place."

Tabor nodded. Then he told Jock how Calahan had

hung his last frame around him. "It's tight, too," he finished. "The timing and everything was perfect."

"Wonder why he didn't just have you done in like he did your brother."

Tabor was silent for a moment, staring out at the light from the street lamps reflecting off the dim-lit store windows. Then he said; "That's not his way. Bill was killed because he had something on Calahan, something big. Me, I don't have anything on him. He knows that and figures I can't do him any harm. So he intends to make me pay the hard way for crossing him. In short, he's showing his power. The only thing he cares about."

Jock glanced at him. "I heard somebody else say that."

"It's true. He doesn't care anything about fine clothes or big cars. None of the things you'd expect a racket boss to like. Only thing he's got that fits the role he's playing is that penthouse. All he cares about is making people squirm, suffer. He loves that."

Fifteen minutes later they were at Jock's place, a neat three-room apartment on the second-floor front of a three-story brownstone walk-up, on North Palmer Street. Jock told him to take the bedroom.

Tabor shook his head at him. "Out here on the studio couch will be just fine. But I could use a steak of some kind if you've got one."

"I don't have one, but I can fix that."

After getting out a tan Palm Beach suit, a dark blue sports shirt, and underclothes and socks for Tabor, Jock went out to get the food.

By the time he got back from the restaurant, Tabor had shaved, showered and dressed. He ate slowly, thinking of Bill's wife and kids. They were going to take Bill's death harder than he did. God! He'd have to see Ruthie.

Suddenly he lost his appetite. Taking a sip of the rye Jock had brought back, he looked across the room where the big guy sat watching him. "Say you found out a couple of things today?"

"Albino—that jive mackman I was telling you about in jail—still has that little chippie Goaldie. Up until this morning he had her stabled up with his other gal that's been peddling it for him for eight-nine years. Rose. That's the other girl's name."

"Know why Goaldie stopped working with this babe Rose all of a sudden?"

Jock pushed his Leghorn to the back of his head, then said, "Well, my guess would be that Arky wants her off the corners until you're in the joint with sixty or seventy years." Taking a small white card from his shirt pocket, he glanced at it and brought it to him. "That's where Albino and Rose stay. I figure if you can catch Albino, you might be able to learn something. He'll blab like a half-looped parrot after a few rabbit punches."

The address was on North Third Street. Tabor dropped the card into his jacket pocket and got to his feet. He clipped the holstered Magnum on his right side and asked Jock if he wanted to use Bill's .38.

Jock grinned. "Man, I got a drawer full of heaters. Brought 'em from Germany after the war." He fingered the keys to the Roadmaster out of his pocket, tossed them to Tabor. "I'd go along, but I'm expecting an important phone call. You can't miss knowing Albino when you see him. He's big and he's a real albino."

Chapter Ten

Tabor parked down the block from Albino's crib and got out and fell in with the mob of jive mackmen, hookers, and winos gay-catting and hustling up and down the broad sidewalk. He walked slowly, watching the faces around him but saw no one he knew.

Albino's crib was two-storied, flat-fronted and jammed against the sidewalk. There were fat fingers of pale light poking through holes in a window shade on the upper floor. The lower floor was dark and windowless. As Tabor was about to step into the dim-lit hallway leading up to Albino's pad, a fly-cat in a yellow pin-striped suit came down the steps. The lad gave him a knowing wink and showed all three of his crumb-crushers in a wide grin. "Man you come to the right place. That sugar's an artist. Believe me, daddy, a stomp-down, good-for-real artist."

Still exposing his three crumb-crushers, the lad pushed into the mob on the sidewalk. Tabor went up the long flight of lopsided stairs, wondering what kind of loving had the babe put on the fly-cat to send him so.

Upstairs he rapped on the only door he saw. He heard a sound and put his ear to one of the dozens of cracks in the door panels. It sounded like somebody in there was gargling. But no one answered.

He knuckled the door again, waited. After a moment or so a feminine voice that sounded like its owner had just finished cutting back the hundred-yard dash in ten seconds flat panted for him to come in.

The fresh red rose was the first thing Tabor saw. He guessed that was because of where it was blossoming. The American Beauty was blossoming from between the twin mounds of a set of melon-sized breasts.

The healthy mounds belonged to a chubby but cute brunette in a pair of white panties and a scanty bra, who sat sprawled in an oversized armchair. The big babe was sweating and breathing hard and sucking hungrily at the neck of an upturned gin bottle.

He didn't see a chair he could park in. So he put his hands behind him, caught the doorknob, and leaned against the door. While the big babe recuperated from the gay-cat's visit, he took a gander about the room. Albino must have been doing something else with the dollars his gals made for him. He sure as hell wasn't dumping them into the upkeep of the place. Comic books strewn on the dirty floor beside a rusty iron bed, lipstick-smeared cigarette butts in a yellowed saucer on a knock-kneed table and a patched rug on the floor made that for sure. The place smelled like a batch of stale sardines.

The brunette gargled some of the liquid around in her mouth and spit in a white chipped porcelain nightpail beside her chair. Then, dabbing at her full lips with the end of a soiled towel draped around her shoulders, she looked up at him with heavy-lidded eyes.

"Cop?" Her voice was slurry, alcohol-heavy.

He shook his head at her, watching the rise and fall of her smooth pink belly. "Albino sent me."

"Oh, a lovin' job."

She sat the gin bottle on the floor, rested her plump arms on the arms of the chair, then appraised him, wriggling her big toes all the while.

He let her look. After a while Albino's big babe smiled. "Sport, I don't know where my man gotcha, but you're all right with me." She got the gin bottle, hit it lightly, and held it out to him. "Take a swig an' name your thrill. A nickel note'll getcha a good wrestlin' job. Two of 'em will getcha the works."

He shook his head on the drink. As he tossed out his first sound, he tried to look embarrassed. He grinned. "You're okay. But I was kinda expecting the other girl."

That had been the wrong thing to say. For a few seconds the babe's healthy breasts stopped undulating. Tabor cursed to himself. The babe lowered the gin bottle to the floor, never once taking her gaze off his face, her heavy-lidded eyes wary.

"Sport, whatcha call yourself puttin' down? My man didn't send you here."

He told the truth. "I'm looking for Goaldie. I've got to find her."

Nothing from the healthy-breasted babe but the same hard stare.

He got out a ten spot, folded it, walked over, and slid it down the top of her bra. He took his time putting it there. She was marshmallow soft. She didn't say anything, didn't even look at his hand, just continued to watch his face. After a moment or so her short fingers began to inch towards the palms of her hands, her sharp fingernails making slow scratching sounds as they dragged over the worn mohair on the arms of the chair. Suddenly a spasm of misery crossed her face and she got to her feet and went to the window overlooking the street.

A long time passed before she asked in a faraway voice: "What did you have to come aroun' here for?"

"To find Goaldie," he said, patting at the sweat on his neck with his handkerchief.

"She ain't here, you can see that. So what're you hanging aroun' for now? Why don't you go?"

"Maybe you can help me."

She tossed her head irritably and came back to the chair, telling him in a hot voice: "I don't have no help for anybody. So now I told you, so now you can get in the wind." Sighing, she dragged a weary hand through her hair and frowned slightly. "The hell with it. The hell with everything." She got her half-filled gin bottle and held it up to the light. "Yep, old bottle, the hell with it, And Miss Rose Carson do mean that to include everything and everybody."

He asked her gently, "Why do you keep hanging on to Albino?"

For a second he thought the girl was going to tell him where to head. Her face tightened. But she just weighted her voice down some more with another jolt from the bottle and looked up at him, her eyes sober, tired.

"He's all I got," she said quietly.

"Would you like a ticket to anywhere you want to go and a nice bankroll in your purse?"

Wariness came into her eyes again. His talk had got out of her range, had got too good to be true. The expression on her face told him she didn't expect to ever have anything but a rusty bed to turn a trick in and a gin bottle to suck on.

"Wouldn't that be nice? Money in your pocket and a ticket to anywhere."

"Anywhere is a mighty big place, sport," she said slowly, "and could cost a lot of money."

He took out his roll, peeled off fifteen bills, and added them to the sawbuck in her bra. "I want to find Albino and Goaldie," he told her then.

The girl wet her lips. Her face had taken on a different expression, one that said here was the big chance, and perhaps the best chance she'd ever have of escaping the misery of a broken-down whore.

"I don't know where Goaldie is. Albino took her away this morning. She might come back, then she might not. He didn't say. Just told me she had too much heat on her and for me to limp out on anybody who comes around asking about her."

"Goaldie act scared? Like maybe she thought Albino was going to hurt her?"

The girl shook her head, and her melon-sized breasts jiggled beautifully. For the first time since entering the house, Tabor felt himself come alive. Raising his gaze from her naked and well-stacked body, he picked a spot between her eyes and stared at it.

"Just how did she act?"

"The little bitch acted like she was glad to go."

"I see." Apparently Calahan didn't figure Goaldie would run off at the mouth about the frame she'd helped work on Tabor. "What's Albino's connection with Calahan?" he asked her.

At that the brunette's face twisted with hatred, "The son-of-a-bitch!" She spat on the floor. "The low-lifed son-of-a-bitch! One of these days I'll kill him!"

"Who? Albino?"

"Arky Calahan, both of them. Every time I hear Arky's name I want to kill him!"

"How come the big hate for Calahan?"

"That's the bastard who's the cause of my being what I am. I was a simple hash slinger, fresh out of a job, when that son-of-a-bitch comes along and fills my empty head with a lot of Hollywood talk. I believed him." Her short laugh had the sound of corn flakes rattling. "God! That bastard seemed so nice. Nobody couldn't of told me Arky wasn't a saint. And after getting a couple of good meals, four or five cheap dresses, and a few dollars from the bastard, I thought he was Mr. Jesus, Himself."

The girl paused, staring down at a spot on the patched rug, biting her lower lip. When she went on her voice was very low.

"One night Arky told me he was throwing a party. When I got there I soon found out I was the honored guest, the lone female among twenty of his hoodlums. Afterwards, they shot craps to see which one would keep me for good."

"And Albino won?"

She nodded slowly. "Albino won. That was eleven years ago. A long time, mister. A long, long time in the gutter." The brunette was silent a moment. Then she let out a long slow breath and said, "Albino's one of Arky Calahan's enforcers. Muscle work is about the only thing he's good for, anyway. Anything that calls for a minimum of brains and a mountain of brawn, get Albino and he'll do a bang-up job."

Tabor asked her, "Where is he now?"

"Chippie chasing. Where else?"

"Any particular stomping ground? Or is he a city-wide chaser?"

"You'll find him in Shipley's Tavern. It's in the next block. South of here. If you don't see him, and some of those jitterbug wenches are there, stick around because he'll be in. That boy's got a snifter like a bloodhound when it comes to finding a piece of penitentiary pork."

He lit up a couple of cigarettes, gave one to the girl and then asked her if she'd known Ritchie Andrews. She nodded, letting smoke trickle from her nostrils. "He was in that twenty-man train at the party Arky threw in my honor. Arky had him killed. At least, that was the word on the grapevine. Ritchie believed it, anyway. When I told him I'd heard Arky was gonna have him bumped, the poor bastard sat up here and went to pieces. Slobbered all over the dump."

Confused, Tabor asked the girl, "What was Ritchie doing here?"

"Hiding out, I think. Nobody told me. But why else would he stay cooped up in this rat hole almost two days, with a fine crib and wife like he had?"

Without a doubt Ritchie had been cooling it. The big question, though, was what the hell had put that kind of heat on the lug, the kind that had forced him to sweat out nearly two days in this room. Ritchie had been a clean cat, a pretty boy, a lover of the brightly lighted sin-dens.

"Did he say anything? Do anything?"

"Uh-huh." The brunette sucked on her cigarette a moment, dropped it into the night-pail, then added, "Nothing but curse the whole world and prowl the floor and listen to the radio. That's all."

"What'd Albino say about it?"

"Oh, he started to squawk. But Ritchie closed his mouth with a few dollars in his slides."

She moved her shoulders and Tabor realized his gaze had slipped down a good ten inches.

Smiling sleepy-eyed at him, the brunette said: "So I still don't know from nothing about what had Ritchie on fire."

He cleared some of the rust out of his throat, mopped up, and said: "He left after you told him you'd heard Calahan was going to have him hit?"

"No, not right away. The slob's knees were shaking so bad he couldn't stand up. Took him a good hour to get himself together. That's when he swooped and a couple of hours later word was out that he'd got it. Run over by a car."

"Think Albino knows what had Ritchie burned up?"

"He might."

He blew out some smoke, then leaned over and tapped a long head of ash off his cigarette into the night-pail, trying hard not to look at Rose's smooth pink stomach.

He said: "As you've probably already guessed, I'm out to smother Calahan's setup, and going by what you've told me, I figure you'd like to see that happen."

"Wouldn't shed a single tear if his whole mob got turned into horse manure," Rose told him emphatically. "Including Albino."

"In that case, would you be willing to stick around few days longer and try to find out where they're keeping Goaldie under wraps?"

"I already made up my mind to do that. Might find you a few other things, too. About Ritchie. How'll I read you if I get something?"

Tabor hesitated, dragging smoke into his lungs. Hell he had to trust somebody. "The phone's under the name of Jock Adams. Ask for Tank."

"I know Jock. A good Joe. Okay, then, I'll call you there if I get a rumor. Thanks for my ticket to anywhere and since one good turn deserves another—" She let it hang there. Her red lips slightly parted, she slowly rubbed her hand back and forth along the inside of her naked thigh.

He shook his head. "You don't owe me anything." He told her good-by and left her sitting there looking up at him as if he were Saint Peter.

After the musky odor up in Albino's place, the air outside smelled fresh. The crowds on the sidewalks hadn't thinned any. If anything, the gay-lifers, the jive mackmen, the hookers, the marks and winos, had multiplied. He got with the mob. Since Shipley's Tavern was only in the next block, he decided to leave the Roadmaster parked.

Then he remembered that every plainclothesman and bluecoat in the city would be on the lookout for him by now. If he kept footing up and down the street, sooner or later someone was going to recognize him.

He changed his mind about leaving the car.

Chapter Eleven

You couldn't read a newspaper in Shipley's Tavern. There wasn't enough light for that, and thirty people would have choked the ratty joint, Tabor figured. It was half-choked now.

Tank satisfied himself that nobody in there could do him much harm. He left the doorway and found a dry spot at the far end of the scarred bar.

"What'll you have, buddy?" a mousy-looking bartender asked, grinning and wiping the bar with a greasy rag.

"Albino been in tonight?" Tabor asked.

The mousy-looking barman's mop-rag didn't stop completely, but Tabor had to lean closer to tell if it was still moving.

"Who's he?"

"A lad we both know," Tabor replied. "I want to see him."

The mop-rag was completely still now. "Who says I know the bird you're talking about?"

"I do," Tabor answered, ignoring the little chippie who brushed against him as she waggled to a stool. "Where can I find him? It's important."

"Since I don't know who you're talking about, buddy, I couldn't say. I—"

The barman's mouth suddenly hung open as if somebody had crammed an orange in it. The screen door had opened and closed and in the peeling mirror in back of the bar Tabor saw his man—Albino. He knew him right away, just as Jock said. The guy, dressed in a blood-red sports coat and white slacks, was big, milky-colored and had bushy hair the color of fresh snow. He was about to go to one of the teenagers in the booths when the barman's voice sliced through the loud music.

"Albino! Cut out!"

It was obvious to Tabor that the barman and Albino had been through this performance before. Without missing a step, or even glancing at them, Albino pivoted and broke for the entrance.

Tabor moved out after him, fast. As he passed the chippies and five greasy-haired fly-cats, one of the fly-cats stuck a foot between his legs. He stumbled but didn't go down. There wasn't time to smack the bastard who had done it.

When Albino hit the screen door, Tabor sailed through the air in a flying tackle. Albino sensed the tackle, jumped to one side, and Tabor belly-flopped on the concrete walk. The wind whooshed out of his lungs but he shot out an arm, got a handful of Albino's ankle and jerked hard.

When the jive mackman smacked against the walk he screamed and tried to roll away. But Tabor crawled all over him, slugging at his milky face with hard lefts and rights. "I'll beat your brains out," he grated. They rolled across the wide sidewalk, taking turns riding and whaling each other.

Then Albino got reinforcements.

The greasy-haired fly-cats and chippies had come out of the joint. The gay-cats stomped at Tabor's head whenever it was on the walk, and whooped at it with beer bottles whenever he showed topside.

He couldn't win that kind of battle, he knew. Heaving hard, he pulled away from Albino. Then he threw up his left hand to block the blows the fly-cats were slinging at his head with the beer bottles, at the same time shucking the Magnum from the clip holster with his right.

One of the chippies shrieked, "He's got a gun!"

One shot in the air was all that was needed. The flycats and chippies dropped their beer bottles and took off in every direction. Albino tried to get in the wind, too, and Tabor swiped at his thin lips with the Magnum. The lad screamed, then spat out teeth and blood.

Crawling over to him, Tabor poked the bore of the Magnum's short barrel in his gut. He glanced around to make sure none of Albino's friends were trying to tip up on him. They weren't. For almost half a block on their side of the street the walk was clean of nightlifers. A crowd had gathered across on the other walk and he saw some of the cats and chippies peeping out of doorways, but none of them wanted any part of the Magnum.

He got his hat, then jerked Albino to a sitting position. He started to ask about the little chippie Goaldie, but he heard shoe leather slapping against the pavement, moving fast, coming their way. He looked toward the sound, then felt the short hairs on the back of his neck get stiff for the second time that night.

Two husky bluecoats were twenty or thirty yards away and he could see light from the street lamps reflecting off the guns in their hands.

Cursing angrily, he dived between two cars at the curb. He got up running. In back of him Albino began shouting, "That guy's Tank Tabor! The guy who murdered his brother this afternoon!"

One of the cops yelled, "Halt, you!"

The Magnum still in his fist, Tabor raced along the row of cars parked along the curb. Jock's Roadmaster was behind him, in front of Shipley's Tavern. He wished he was in it and on his way out of the neighborhood. One of the patrolmen back there was after a promotion. He cut loose with his heater and

Tabor heard the slug bite viciously into the side of the car he was passing.

Taking a quick glance behind him, he saw the cop out in the middle of the street, down on one knee, taking careful aim. The sidewalk was no better. The other cop bore down on him and he was promotion-bent too. His gun cracked three times. Lead scorched past Tabor's ear, tugged at his hat brim.

There was nothing else he could do, no other way out if he wanted to make the gangway he was headed for without getting riddled. Whirling suddenly, he blasted the air over the cop's head. The cop beat it into the hallway and he made the gangway, but he knew he was worse off now than ever. The shot he'd flung the cop's way would bring orders from the brass downtown, for every cop in the city to cut him down on sight.

As hot as the night was, an icy feeling crawled through his heaving chest.

He triple-timed through an apron of bright light coming from the side entrance of the building on his right, listening for the sound of the cops' footsteps, but the only shoe leather he could hear slapping against concrete was his own. After that shot he'd fired they'd probably phone in for reinforcements.

Breaking out into the yard behind the building, he halted suddenly. He stared. Then panic hit him.

There was a brick wall at least fifteen feet high around the yard and light from a naked bulb over the exit showed him the heavy-duty lock on the steel gate that opened into the alley. He sleeved sweat out of his eyes, looked back the way he'd come, then hit the ground just as the cop fired.

He rolled away from the gangway onto the grass and then scampered to the gate to see if he was lucky.

He wasn't. The heavy steel gate was locked tight.

He stepped back and fired at the big lock. There was a lot of noise when the lock slammed against the gate but the lock didn't open. He blasted it again. It disintegrated; its pieces ricocheted off the steel gate and flew all over the yard. He wanted to kiss the Magnum. Working feverishly, he got the gate open. He was about to lunge out into the alley when he heard a tin can rattle and then a low, angry, "Quiet, damn it!"

He battled down the urge to bolt out into the alley, anyway. That would be begging to get it. For anyone out there who could shoot even a little bit, getting him would be easy—like puncturing an inflated weather balloon with a shotgun at ten feet.

With a hand that was running water he eased the gate shut, screwed out the light over it, and looked around. There wasn't too much worry in him about anyone rushing him. They knew he had a gun. But he knew he had to get out of there before more law got on the scene or his gun would do nothing but get him chopped down if he tried to use it. And a sound he had begun to hate, the baying of a siren, told him the cops were not too far away.

Lights had come on in most of the houses along the alley and he saw several danger-lovers hanging far out of windows, trying to see what was happening. He moved away from the gate, keeping to the soft grass, and got down on his belly to peep around the corner of the building toward the front. One of the cops, crouched down and tipping like a ballet dancer, was in the gangway.

Tabor threw a shot over the cop's head and watched him break a gangway-dash record getting back out front. Then he got up off his belly, sprinted to the brightly lighted side entrance of the building, and ducked inside.

The hall was long and dim with white-knobbed doors on either side of it and smelled like somebody on the floor was cooking liver and onions. Taking a chance on bolting out the front way had been in his mind, but human shadows showing through the half-glassed door of the entrance made him change his mind. He looked at the tight stairs that wound up into the building, listening to the baying of the siren getting closer. More sweat popped out of his scalp. He could feel it sliding down his neck.

A door on his left creaked open and he spun around, bringing up the Magnum. A bright-eyed young blonde tomato in a tight-fitting housecoat stood inside the dim-lit doorway. When she saw Tabor her hands flew to her throat and her bright eyes stretched wide. She opened her mouth to scream. Then she sort of sighed, her eyes rolling up in her head, and crumpled to the floor in a dead faint.

Tabor stepped inside the semi-dark room, which he saw was a small kitchen. He leaned down and moved the blonde from in front of the door.

Heeling the door shut, he crouched there beside the blonde, his ears perking. The light spilling into the kitchen was coming from a bedroom on the far side of the building. A corner of a low bed showed through the cracked door but he couldn't tell if anybody was in it. The house was quiet.

Straightening up, he skirted the blonde's legs and moved toward the light. The air in the house, like the air outside, was hot and oppressive. The hand gripping the Magnum was slimy with sweat. Even if the babe wasn't married it wasn't likely that she slept by herself very much. She was too cute and had too many curves in the right places for the lads around this neighborhood to let her do a silly thing like that too often.

The sweet thing hadn't been sleeping by herself tonight.

When he toed the bedroom door open he saw a gray-headed guy standing on one leg struggling to get into a pair of crimson polka-dot shorts.

At the sight of him the old boy froze with his foot still cocked. For a second or two they stared at each other. The old boy gawked at the gaping bore of the Magnum and started shaking and blubbering.

"God, mister, don't shoot! I didn't know! She told me she was single, ask her. I—"

"Easy, pops," Tabor said, stepping into the room. "Don't mind me, I'm just passing through. But I wish you wouldn't holler when I leave."

"I won't, son. I won't. God knows I won't!"

"Thanks." Tabor saw his luck wasn't all bad. There was a green-shaded window across the room facing the backyard of the house next door. He walked over and stood to one side of it. The window was already up and he could hear the siren baying, closer now, much closer. He slanted a glance at the old man, who was working feverishly to get into his shorts.

"Easy, pops. How many fences between here and the corner?"

"Three."

"Low or high?"

"Low."

Tabor began breathing again. "All right, pops, go on and knock yourself out."

He reached over the bed and pulled the light string, blackening out the room. Then, lifting the shade, he cautiously slid a leg over the window sill. There he paused. Nobody yelled. Nobody shot at him.

He climbed on through the window to the ground. For a moment he crouched there listening and looking down the row of buildings. The danger-lovers were still hanging out of their windows. Out front a siren was dying and he knew at least one car of cops had arrived. It was time for him to quit the scene.

His eyes searching the ground for rubbish piles, he crept across the yard, keeping close to the flat backs of the buildings. He'd made two of the three fences the old guy told him about when a low-voiced dame hollered down at him from a second-floor window of the building he was creeping past. "Hey you. What the hell you doing in my yard?"

Still moving toward the last fence, Tabor came out of his crouch. "Just taking a short cut," he told her. He wished she'd keep her jaws shut.

She didn't. She got louder. "Well, you just short cut someplace else, mister. Last time one of you bums short-cutted through my yard at night, I was short of four good window screens the next morning."

Ignoring the dame, he started over the fence left between him and the corner, between him and his only chance to get the hell away from there.

The grating voice sounded off again. "Hey you. How come you don't use the gate?" The voice picked up volume with every word. "Hey, you. Go—" The dame cut out loud-talking and began to scream. "Hey, everybody! Here he is, that bum you're hunting for! Here he is in my yard!"

There were shouts all around Tabor from more of the danger-lovers as he clambered over the fence. He dug in and ran for the corner, listening to more sirens dying out front. Somebody hanging out of one of the windows tried to scramble his brains with a jug but it missed him and shattered on the top of a garbage can.

Making the corner, he cut around it and headed for the Roadmaster. Maybe in the excitement he'd be able to get away with it. As he came to Third Street three prowl cars whipped around the corner. Each one was clogged to its ceiling light with law. He slowed to a walk and tried to keep his chest from heaving so fast. The prowl cars rolled on down the block toward the mob of noisy excitement-hounds in the street, their sirens doing a slow fade, the red spots on their tops blinking and turning slowly from side to side.

So far as Tabor could tell nobody had connected him with the Roadmaster. At least no one was around the car. Walking casually, his hand shoved deep into his pants pocket, the Panama pushed to the back of his head, he got close to the curb, out of the light splashing from the joints, and advanced toward Shipley's Tavern. The excitement had emptied most of the joints. When the prowl cars halted, he thought they would never get done puking cops.

He rubbed sweat from his forehead with the back of his hand, glanced up at the star-bright sky. He wished the night was less hot and much blacker.

When he reached the Roadmaster he didn't waste any time getting in. The danger-lovers out back were yelling loud enough to wake up everybody in the city. As he started the car he looked at Shipley's Tavern. The mousy-looking barman was standing in the doorway, peering at him.

Chapter Twelve

When Tabor pulled off he glanced at the rearview mirror and saw the barman hot-footing toward the prowl cars, frantically waving his arms in the air.

He made a right turn at the first corner he came to, sped three blocks, made another right turn at Sixth Street. There was no traffic to worry about and Sixth was a one-way street, so he stuck his foot in the

Roadmaster's gas tank. For fifteen blocks he had everything his way. He kept the speedometer needle fanning eighty.

The Roadmaster would be too hot for him to ride in from now on, he knew. The bartender had had plenty of time to look at the car. He didn't think the guy had got the license number, though.

He made a couple more turns, then headed for Jock's place. Arky Calahan was the cause of all this, he thought bitterly. But why? What was Calahan afraid of? So far he'd learned absolutely nothing. And Calahan and the cops were steadily closing in, steadily tightening the net around him.

The sirens were baying again, but they weren't close. He drew up before Jock's place, turned off the ignition and lights, and got out of the car, locking the door behind him. Most of the brownstones along the block were dark, quiet, and the sidewalks were deserted.

When he got upstairs, Jock was standing in his doorway, waiting for him. The big guy's wise eyes took in his roughed-up appearance, but he didn't start slinging a lot of questions at him. Tabor appreciated that. He walked past him and dropped into the deep chair and sat staring blankly in front of him, wondering what to do next and trying to keep Monkey Face Moe off his mind. If he kept thinking about that freakish son-of-a-bitch, about the way he'd shot up Bill, he knew he'd go hunting for him and would cut him down wherever he found him.

Jock closed the door, walked over to an end table beside the studio couch, and snapped off the small radio on it. "Those people," he said, indicating the radio with a sideward motion of his head. "The Mad-Dog Killer, that's what they're calling you now."

Tabor nodded and stretched his legs out in front of him. He looked at the gold watch on his wrist. Ten after twelve. Then he told Jock about his car being hot.

Jock shook his head. He picked up the bottle of rye he'd bought earlier and unscrewed the top. "They don't know much about it. I heard the flash over the radio— that juice-jerker that saw you quitting the scene didn't know much about cars. All he could say was the car you left in was long and black." Jock brought him one of the tall glasses he had poured half full of rye. "Of course we got to act like maybe that fellow got everything from the color to the motor number, because the cops are old pros when it comes to giving out misleading information. They make a guy think he's safe and the minute he shows on the scene they snatch all the fat out of him. They may be trying to do that in this case."

"Could be," Tabor agreed, and then told him about giving Rose his phone number. "Think she'll let Albino know I'm holing up here when she finds out the cops want me?"

"Not hardly. That girl hates Albino. I can't figure why she stuck with him all this time."

The girl's words came to Tabor's mind, and he could think of no better answer. "He was all she had," he said.

Jock shrugged and dropped down on the studio couch. Tabor took a big swallow of his drink. The rye let him know some of Albino's blows had cut the inside of his lower lip. The lip burned. A sore spot on the left side of his face and a marble-sized lump on his knowledge knot told him the lad and his jitter-bop friends had also done other damage. He looked at his hat. There was a small nick along the edge of the brim. Another couple of inches to the right and that cop would have earned his promotion.

Jock said: "Did they come that close?"

He nodded. Drink in hand, he went to the bathroom and inspected his face in the small mirror over the wash bowl. Blood from a slight cut along his left cheek bone had crusted on his face. He washed off the blood, rinsed out his mouth, then fouled it up again with the rest of the rye in the glass. Then he brushed off his clothes. In his rumble with Albino, Jock's suit hadn't been ruined, just got a little dirty.

On the way out of the bathroom he thought of how Albino had shattered a track record of some kind getting to the door when the mousy-looking barman in Shipley's shouted for him to cut out. The guy had been in such a hurry to swoop that he hadn't even taken time to look and see who he was swooping from.

That lad's got a lot on his conscience, he thought.

Back in the living room he serviced the Magnum, dropped a handful of bullets for it into his jacket pocket. Then he went across the room to where the phone stood on a small oblong table in the corner and dialed Kate Lamain's number. As nasty as it was, the thought that she might have set him up so Calahan could frame him with Bill's murder was still slithering through his mind. He wanted to make sure she hadn't. When she came to the phone, he said: "Kate, Tank."

Her long sigh sounded as if it was a sigh of relief. "Tank, darling, I'm sorry about Bill." Her voice was choked. "Now Arky is—"

He broke in on her. "Did you know Moe was going to be in my apartment waiting for me when you bailed me out of jail?"

"Tank!" she cried, and then was silent for so long he thought she had left the phone. He waited, watching Jock on the other side of the room as the big guy sipped his drink and studied him over the rim of the glass.

"I asked you a question," he reminded her finally.

"I heard it, Tank." Kate spoke quietly. "We're going to have a heck of a battle about that crack, but that has to wait. Right now, I want you to go help Tess."

His hand tightened around the phone. "Tess?"

"Yes. A girlfriend of mine who hangs out in Arky's bar called just now and told me some of his boys are up at Tess's apartment giving her a going over, trying—"

He didn't wait to hear the rest of Kate's talk. He dropped the receiver in its cradle and ran to the front door, his breath loud and harsh in his throat.

"What's the play?" Jock asked, as Tabor fumbled with the lock on the door with shaky hands.

"Some of Calahan's hoods are roughing up Tess." He saw Jock bound to his feet and run into his bedroom, then he was out in the hall, taking the steps three and four at a time. He cursed himself for not realizing Calahan would try to get him to raise up off the case by pushing Tess.

When he got the Roadmaster unlocked, Jock was right behind him. It took them twelve minutes to cover the ten miles to Tess's place. On the way they had worked out a plan. They knew there would be a stakeout around someplace and that had to be quietly taken care of before they tried for the guys upstairs.

A couple of cars were parked in front of Tess's building, but Tabor didn't see anybody in them. That didn't mean anything, he thought, looking both ways along the quiet street. The gangways that he could see were dark and seemingly empty, too.

He glanced at Jock who had slumped down in the seat until he was out of sight from anyone outside. "Here goes."

"Okay," Jock whispered. "Just do a little talking to cover any noise I might make."

When Tabor got out of the car he stopped under the

gleaming canopy over the entrance of Tess's building and fired up a cigarette, trying to act as if his nerves were not as tight as high-tension telegraph wires. He flipped the match stem on the lawn. Then, pulling at his cigarette, he took a slow step forward, straining his ears, trying to catch some sound from the stakeout.

He caught a sound. And it hadn't been necessary to strain his ears to catch it. The keen voice that came from behind him was plenty plain.

"Slow down, Tank," the keen voice lisped. "All the way down."

Tabor recognized the voice. It belonged to Wally, a gay-dressing young hood who had more than a little bit of lavender in him. He started to turn around and Wally lisped again.

"You better keep still, Tank, or I'll give it to you right here on the street."

Tabor stopped. "I'll give you a grand to close your eyes for a couple of minutes and let me go on upstairs," he said, keeping up the chatter. "A fat grand for doing nothing. You couldn't do better than that in Reno and they're known to give some pretty good deals out there. Just think of all the yellow shoes, orange shirts, and red slacks you could buy with ten bills. You could get pretty as hell with all that money."

"Tank, I'm not holding still for your spiel." Wally tee-heed. "I don't hafta. I'll take the money off your corpse."

Tabor heard footsteps crossing the walk, then felt the bore of what he knew was a gun poke him in his spinal column and smelled Wally's cologne.

"Don't get excited." Outwardly, he was controlled, but his spine was tingling like a plucked banjo string. "You don't have to jump hog-wild to get the dough. You can have it without a rumble."

There was a grunt from Wally and Tabor felt the gun slide down his back and, a second later, heard it clatter on the walk. Without looking back, he ran into the vestibule and started pushing the bells of all the apartments above Tess's. Sweat was pouring from his scalp again, sliding down his face. Through the glass in the door he saw Jock drag Wally feet first across the walk and stuff him into the back seat of one of the cars parked in front of the building.

He wished the people would get up to answer their doors. Tight-lipped, he flung his cigarette into the sand urn beside the door, then went back to punching bells. Jock, hatless and shoeless, came into the vestibule, shoving a long-barreled .38 under his belt. There was a hardness in the big guy's eyes Tabor had never seen in them before. He was glad they were friends.

"Look," he said suddenly, as a new and better idea hit him. "We'll junk our original plan. I got a better one. That's if you're willing to front the gun."

"Tell me the score," Jock said softly. "Tess is my friend, too."

Tabor told him the score.

Jock nodded to let him know he'd got the play, then thumbing over his shoulder at the car he'd stuffed Wally's limp form in, he said; "I couldn't chance trying to take him out in talking condition. I know that freak-o. He would've tried to blast his way out if I hadn't cooled him."

"Think he'll sleep long?"

"We'll have time."

One of the tenants upstairs finally buzzed, and he watched as Jock propped open the door with the sand urn, took out his Luger, and trotted to the self-service elevator.

Tabor listened to the elevator hum its way upstairs with the big guy.

Now, he thought, getting Calahan's hoods to open the door for Jock was his part in the play.

The elevator came down again. Now there were things to be done. Three or four times he practiced Wally's lisp. Then he pressed Tess's bell. His pump was kicking hard at his ribs. A loud coarse voice bellowed through Tess's speaker. "Goddamn it, what the hell's the matter with you, Wally. Can't you quit leaning on that bell?"

"There's a kid down here looking for Tess," Tabor lisped, hoping he was getting a lot of Wally into his voice. "Tank sent him, I think. The little bastard's trying to get away. Come down and get him."

"Hang on to him a sec. I'll send one of the boys down."

The run to the elevator was the longest short run Tabor had ever made in his life. Once inside, he stabbed the button for the fourth floor, then checked the Magnum. The elevator seemed like it was making the climb in slow motion. As it approached the fourth floor he heard a gun go off, firing four shots. He flinched.

When the elevator jarred to a stop he was out in the hall running for Tess's apartment before the cage door had opened all the way. There was a man sprawled on the rug just inside Tess's door and Tabor breathed easier when he saw it wasn't Jock.

With the Magnum cocked he leaped into the apartment and moved quickly to one side. But nobody took a shot at him. The furniture in the high-ceilinged living room was scrambled up. The white plush sectional sofa lay upside down, its stuffing hanging out of its split bottom. One end of the deep-napped rug was turned back and the soft floor pillows slit, the cotton stuffing strewn about the floor.

But nobody was in the room. No Tess. No Jock. Nobody but the guy sprawled on the rug in front of the door and he didn't look like he was in this world any longer. Tabor didn't see how the guy could be, with half of his head blown off the way it was.

Toeing the door shut as he passed, he ran to Tess's bedroom. He stood to one side of the half-open door. The bedroom had been wrecked, too. Drawers from a highboy had been pulled out and some underclothes been thrown into a corner. He eased the door open all the way and what he saw twisted his mind. Made him want to commit murder.

Tess was in there, stretched spread-eagle on her bed, naked, her wrists and ankles tied to the bedposts. He whirled around, half-blind with a destructive rage, and ran through a short hall that ended at Tess's kitchen. His breath was harsh, ragged in his throat.

Jock was coming back through the kitchen door and Tabor stopped. "Three got away," he said, breathing hard and speaking rapidly. His cocoa-brown face was tight and shiny with sweat. "Get Tess and get out of here. Use this way to go down. I'll get the guy they left behind. We better hurry."

Tabor snatched a sharp knife out of a rack beside the sink. "Don't wait for us. We'll use Tess's car." He let the hammer down and holstered his gun as he trotted back to the bedroom.

Tess wasn't out, but she didn't look at him as he cut her loose. Her eyes were shut tightly, but tears squeezed from under her lids and rolled slowly down her milk-white cheeks. She kept moving her head from side to side on the pillow.

Tess opened her eyes. She looked at him blankly for a moment, as if she were coming from under a heavy dose of ether.

"It's me, honey, Tank," he said gently. "We have to get out of here."

She nodded her head slowly. "All right, Tank." Her voice was low, tired, like that of a weary battlefront nurse. Like a sleepwalker, she got up, slid back the door of a built-in closet, snapped on a light, and took down a black silk dress from the crowded clothes rack.

Beneath the array of dresses, suits and coats Tabor saw several pieces of cowhide luggage. He got out the two largest pieces and crammed them with dresses and shoes from the closet and underclothes from the pile in the corner. As he closed the bags he thought of Calahan and his hoods. Trying to get them legally was out now. He'd play the game their way.

From out in the living room came the sound of furniture being moved. Jock was taking the rug, he figured.

Smart boy. Without the big guy's help he'd have been well up that well-known creek by now.

By the time he got the bags fastened Tess was dressed and waiting for him. She stood beside the highboy, one clenched fist resting on top of a white leather purse that hung from her shoulder, staring at the opposite wall as if she were looking through it.

"Got your car keys?" he asked her.

Without looking at him she opened her purse, dipped her hand into it, and came out with her keys. After giving them to him she snapped the purse together and said tonelessly: "The money those men wanted is in the kitchen stove, in a paper bag."

He got the two pieces of luggage and followed her out into the living room. The hood's body and the deep-napped rug were gone. At least he had the satisfaction of knowing that one of Calahan's punks wouldn't be trying to push them anymore. Thanks to Jock. He heard a muted sound of voices out in the hall. He wondered if the cops would break into the apartment when they got here and nobody answered the door. It was a good bet that they would. Those shots had to be accounted for.

Chapter Thirteen

They had no trouble getting away from Tess's place. Tabor drove slowly through the hot and humid night toward Jock's apartment, careful of all traffic signs. Tess sat quietly beside him, staring through the window on her side, struggling to hang on to her control.

It was one-fifteen when he parked Tess's Continental up the street from Jock's apartment building and got out. In silence, they walked toward the brownstone. Jock's Roadmaster was in front of the house and the lights in both the living room and the bedroom were on in his apartment.

Jock had the door open for them when they got upstairs. His eyes hadn't softened any—that Tabor could see. The big guy had his jacket off and there was a smudge of dust on his shirt sleeve.

"Put her bags in the bedroom," he told Tabor. "I just changed the linens on the bed and cleaned the room up a bit."

When the suitcases had been deposited in the bedroom, Tabor made drinks and drank his slowly, letting the rye burn its way all the way to his stomach. The cuts inside his lower lip that he'd gotten in his fight with Albino started acting up. He let them burn. The pain was a stimulant, kept his mind alive. He sat on the studio couch beside Jock and looked at Tess huddled in the deep chair on the other side of the room, her rust-colored hair a glistening halo around her sad but beautiful face. As he looked at her he felt a strong flow of tenderness move him.

"Tank," Tess said softly, her eyes looking down at the untouched drink in her hand, "I want to take a bath."

Jock said: "The bath's right off the bedroom. The lights are already on and clean towels are in there."

"Thanks, Jock," Tess said, still not looking up. "Thanks to both of you."

After she had gone, taking her drink with her, Tabor asked Jock: "Who were the others?"

"Moe, Trigger Slim and Croaker. Shot at 'em a couple of times, but missed."

Tabor checked his gun. "Got any idea where they hang out?" he asked quietly.

The big guy looked at him a long time, taking slow sips of his drink. After a while he nodded. "At Arky's bar. Only the kind of thinking you're doing now, man, is all crazy."

"Maybe. But I'm done playing cop. From here on in I'm playing the way I know how to play."

After that the room was quiet. Jock made patterns on one of the cushions on the couch with one big finger as if reluctant to speak his next words. Then shaking his head slowly, he said softly: "You're not thinking now, man. You're all twisted up. Ready to flip—I feel the same way. I think a lot of your girl Tess and will do everything I can to get back at Arky's flunkies for raping her. Only if we go slamming into Arky's joint now, we'd get smothered with lead before we got through the door. Tank, you know Arky'll be waiting for us with a joint full of gun-heavy punks."

Tabor didn't say anything. About five fingers of rye were left in the bottle. He picked it up. When he took the neck of the bottle out of his glass less than two fingers of juice were left in the bottle. Jock was right, but he had to let out some of the hell that was boiling inside him, or he'd crack. He downed the rye and set the empty glass on the table.

Jock picked up the bottle, looked at him. When Tabor

shook his head, Jock emptied the rest of the rye into his own glass and said: "Okay. So we go out and get smothered. How will that leave Tess? Who'll take Arky off her back then?"

"You're right," he admitted. "I've junked the plan." He reached into his jacket pocket for a cigarette and felt the paper bag with Tess's dough in it. He hadn't looked in the bag, but he figured it was the thirty-five G's she drew out of the bank to get him out on bail. A lump formed in his throat.

"Trigger Slim and them see you?"

"I'm not sure," Jock said. "At least I don't know if any of 'em saw me well enough to recognize me."

"What happened to the guy they left behind?"

Jock frowned. "Dumped him behind Arky's poolroom. I gassed and burned the rug."

Tabor continued to look at him and he was smiling now. "Like to play on the underdog's team, don't you? Lucky for me you are." He inhaled deeply, let the smoke dribble from his nose. His stomach cut up a time or two and he realized he was hungry again. He was about to ask Jock about putting in a supply of food when he heard Tess crying. She wasn't crying loud. Her sobs were muffled, as if she had her face buried in a pillow.

Tabor snuffed out his cigarette, silently damning Calahan, and got to his feet.

"I'd better go to her. You in for the night?"

"Uh-uh. Think I'll make a few of the crap houses. Might pick up a word we can use." Jock took a key off a ring he brought from his pocket and gave it to him. "That's an extra key to the door. Oh yes, I gave Tess the key to your place."

When Tabor entered the dimly lighted bedroom, he saw Tess curled up on the bed, her face pressed into a pillow. The muffled sobs that shook her body twisted something in him. He sat on the side of the bed and put his hands on her shoulders. "Tess," he whispered, gently lifting her until her head rested on his chest. "Easy does it, hon."

"Oh, Tank! It was terrible," Tess choked out. "Th—they ra—ra—"

He patted her shoulder. "Don't try to tell me about it now. Get some sleep."

Her arms went around his neck, and he could feel every sob that shook her body. Decision came to him then. Monkey Face Moe and Trigger Slim had to go.

After a while Tess stopped crying. She pulled him down on the bed, snuggling against him like a little girl seeking the comforting safety of her father's arms.

Tabor didn't know how long he had slept. But it must not have been long because darkness still hugged the city outside when he awoke to the jangling of the phone. Tess stirred in his arms, but didn't wake up. Still groggy with sleep, he eased his arm from under her neck and lumbered out to the living room, noticing as he passed the studio couch that Jock hadn't come in.

"Yeah?" he yawned into the mouthpiece.

"Tank?" a slurry feminine voice asked.

Tabor perked up. The slurry voice belonged to Albino's girl, Rose. "Yeah, girlfriend. What's happening?"

"I heard about your rumble with Albino. Still want that chat with him?"

"Bad."

"Okay, well, listen then. Know the alley down from the house? From my house?"

"Yeah."

"Well, midway dawn the alley is a junkyard. Go an' wait in the hall of the building on the east side of the junkyard; it's a dope pad and our boy'll be creeping in there to get his nightly speed in about fifteen or twenty minutes. Got that?"

"Yeah. Thanks, honey."

"Gotta run now."

They said goodbye, and Tabor cradled the receiver, looking across the room to where Tess stood in the doorway of the bedroom knuckling sleep from her eyes. She had slipped on a white silk robe that ruffled neatly into the lush curves of her body.

He went over and took her hands in his. They were warm and soft.

"I have to go out for a little while, hon."

She nodded. Without make-up, her face was wan, but her chin was firm, and her big blue eyes clear and unafraid.

"Jock gone?"

"Yeah." He nodded toward the chair beside the window where Bill's snub-nose .38 lay. "Keep that gun with you. If you have to use it don't forget what I used to tell you all the time. Either try to bust his heartstring or blow his brains out so you won't have to worry about him anymore."

Tess shivered. For a moment they stood looking into each other's eyes. Then, before he knew how it had happened, they were hugging and kissing each other hungrily. He was having trouble with his breathing and Tess was making little cooing sounds in her throat. Tabor was back home again and he was glad. He was glad all over.

Chapter Fourteen

Without the neons lighting the joints and the jukeboxes blaring and the fly-cats and kittens and winos and squares frolicking up and down the wide walks, Third Street was just another dismal-looking slum street. To a guy not in the know it would seem that all the sin peddlers and buyers had crawled into their respective cribs for the morning. But Tabor knew better. Nothing had been changed but the locations. In the smoky dim-lit back rooms and basements the cats and kittens and squares were still playing, the kittens selling it to the squares and putting it on the cats just for kicks.

He checked the time. Three-forty. He'd made the run in eight minutes and he wondered if he'd been rushing into a trap. There was only one way to find out. But he hoped he wasn't, hoped the brunette hadn't sold him out to Arky Calahan.

Before he turned into the alley Rose had instructed him to, he looked back down the block to where he'd parked Tess's car. Sitting there alone, the Continental looked lonely, and so far away.

Turning, he unlimbered his gun and then started up the pitch-black alley. He cursed softly when his right foot squished down into a pile of wet, stinking garbage.

Finally, he made the building next to the junkyard the brunette had told him about. The dope pad. His eyes had accustomed themselves to the inky darkness and he could make out the outline of a door. Who—if anyone—was on the other side of the door was the question worrying him now.

For a while he stood there listening. No sounds but

the far-off noises of the city came to him, an off-key horn, a speeding car, and closer by but still far away, the deep growl of a motor bus. Nothing stirred in the alley.

Rose had directed him to wait inside the hallway. Why? Why not in the alley? It crossed his mind to disregard the brunette's instructions and plan his own campaign. He knuckled his chin thoughtfully. If he went against the girl's instructions, he might muff his chance of grabbing Albino, if she'd been leveling with him. Perhaps she'd had a good reason for specifically telling him to wait in the hallway.

He stood to one side and tried the door. It was unlocked. Drawing in a deep breath, he crouched low and quickly shoved the door open all the way. It squeaked like hell. A blob of dull red light splashed over him, but that was all. No bullets. The long hallway was empty. Maybe Rose had given him a pure tip after all.

He straightened up and stepped inside the building and eased the door shut, feeling a light coating of fresh sweat on the backs of his hands. The brunette had said Albino would be creeping in to get his shot of junk in fifteen or twenty minutes. He peered at his watch. Fourteen minutes had gone by since then. He moved over to the wall behind the door and waited. The air in the hallway was still muggy from the heat of the day and almost as smelly as the alley. Somewhere in the upper part of the decaying structure a radio or record player was churning out "Only A Moment Ago." The babe chirping the number had tears in her voice.

Then Tabor jerked his head toward the door, listening. Had the noise he'd heard been footsteps? Out in the alley a dog yapped twice, then fell silent again. He relaxed and put away the Magnum. He was about to take a smoke when the hall door swung open.

For a second both of them froze up, staring at each other. Then Albino was crouching and clawing under his jacket with wild speed. Tabor, whipping his coat away from the Magnum, drew and lashed out at his chin with his foot, all in one motion. The foot cracked under Albino's chin, bringing him up to his toes, and he forgot about what he'd been clawing for under his jacket and went down grabbing for the sky, letting out a strained cry. Before he could get over the effect of one shoe, Tabor jumped and landed in his face with two more. Albino threw one hand up to his face and screamed he had broken his jaw but he was grabbing under his jacket again with the other hand. Tabor whirled around and slashed him across the face with the Magnum just as the hall door shut, blocking off the light. The guy stopped screaming and grabbing.

Tabor fell all over him, just in case he was shamming. It was too dark in the alley to see anything. Albino didn't struggle so he slid a hand under his coat to see what he'd been scratching for. He didn't see it, but he felt it. There was a man-sized automatic in his hip pocket. Lights came on in several of the buildings as he snatched the gun out and threw it across the alley. Getting a fistful of jacket collar, he dragged Albino's heavy body into the hall and closed the door.

Jock had said the boy might talk behind a head whipping, he remembered. He smiled tightly. With his ears tuned to pick up approaching footsteps he put away his gun, then propped Albino against the wall. The whack across the mouth he'd given him with the Magnum hadn't done him any good, either. His lips were raggedy and swollen and there was a half-inch gap where two upper teeth should have been. Tabor began smacking him back and forth across his slack jaws, not hard blows, just with enough sting in them to wake the punk up.

"Come out of it, clown," he grated. Globs of sweat rolled down his neck. He let it roll and kept smacking.

Albino came out of it after a while. Whimpering, he ducked his head and tried to cover his face with his hands. Tabor let up on the smacking. "Be nice and maybe I won't scramble your brains."

Then he asked about a couple of things that had been on his mind since Calahan framed him with Bill's murder. "Among other things, I want to know is—where'd your cronies catch my brother and when?"

Albino studied Tabor, his pink lips wrinkling in a sneer.

"Go to hell!"

Tabor hit him. The force of the blow twisted Albino's head sideways.

"Talk," Tabor said without emotion.

The big albino ran his tongue over his swollen lips, watching him. Suddenly he shoved him back and broke for the door.

Waiting until he was reaching for the knob, Tabor cow-kicked him in the bend of the leg, knocking him to his knees. Albino's head cracked into the door. Remembering what the punk was making Rose do caused hell to bust loose in Tabor's swelling chest. He jerked Albino to his feet, backed him against the wall, and tried to finish wrecking his jaw with a hard right hook.

Before the albino could fall, he yanked him erect.

"Talk."

There was blood spilling from Albino's mouth and his breath gurgled in his throat. In a whimpering voice, after spitting out clots of blood on the floor, he began to talk, his pink eyes watching Tabor's carefully.

"Moe an' Slade got your brother in front of your apartment door, I heard. Don't know exactly what time. Sometime in the morning, I think."

Probably Bill had been at his place trying to dig up some evidence that would have cleared him of those phony charges, Tabor thought. He asked Albino, "Who's Slade?"

"The guy you an' your buddy wasted last night."

"They get anything from my brother?"

"I dunno for sure. I heard Moe phoned Arky from your hotel when they got your brother an' Arky told him to make your brother open up." Albino shook his head. There was begrudging admiration in his voice. "Only your brother don't open up. He holds out against Moe an' Slade all day. So when Arky gets the wire Kate's going your bail, he sends Trigger Slim over to your place to tell Moe to bump your brother. An' how to put you in the fiddle for it. That's the way I heard it."

That made Tabor feel proud. At least Bill had stayed honest, had stuck to his beliefs, against all pressures. The kid had been a little scared maybe, but not gutless.

"Where's Goaldie?"

A ball of fear sweat rolled down between Albino's eyes and hung from the top of his nose. "Arky got her. He had me bring her to him this morning. That's the truth."

"She at his place?"

Albino nodded.

"Okay, now," Tabor said, "tell me about Ritchie Andrews. What was his reason for holing up in your crib and why'd Calahan have you bastards knock him off?"

That brought Albino's head up sharply. His pink eyes were alive with raw fear. For a while he said nothing, just searched Tabor's face intently, as if trying to make up his mind about something, unmindful of the blood dribbling from his slack mouth and staining his shirt. At length he came alive. He clutched Tabor's arm excitedly and began blubbering.

"I don't know nothin' about what Ritchie was running from. Or why he got hisself killed. But I got something else. Only if Arky finds out about this it could get me hit. But I'm gonna give it to you anyhow. Just gimme a chance to quit the scene is all I ask. That ain't too much to give for what I got."

"Talk. We'll see."

Albino sleeved gore off his mouth, cut a frightened glance toward the door, then brought his gaze back to Tabor. "Arky sent some of the boys out to get Kate Lamain a while ago."

"No!" Tabor breathed the word. Ready to explode, he grabbed a fistful of Albino's shirt and twisted. "You're shoveling con at me to get the weight up off your back." His voice throbbed with violence. "Tell me you're lying."

Albino shook his head quickly. "But I ain't. I'm telling you straight news. Like he wanted to do with Tess Andrews, Arky's gonna use Kate to try to get you outta his hair. Heard him say this just a little while ago. I—" Tabor didn't hear the rest. He'd jerked open the door and was stumbling out into the dark, garbage-strewn alley. He ran toward the Continental, his breath harsh in his throat. Somebody shouted at him from one of the buildings. He ignored it. He was a fool for not insisting that Kate go down to Chicago until this mess was cleaned up. God! He hoped Calahan's hoods hadn't got to her yet. Maybe he could get her away from her place before they did.

Chapter Fifteen

From Third Street he sped to an all-night chili house on Walnut Street and dialed Kate's number in a booth. He listened to the phone jangling in her house for a long time. Nobody answered. Tabor slammed the receiver on the hook and got out of there.

At somewhere around a quarter of five he was easing the key Kate had given him into the front door of her house. The rancho was dark. He stood to one side and gave the door a push. It opened all the way, on silent hinges. He listened, but heard only the chirping of crickets and, every few seconds, faintly and far away, the baying of a hound.

Tabor drew in a slow breath of the fragrant air, then eased inside the house. He closed the door and called Kate's name.

No answer, no sound at all within the cool house. The thick silence was foreboding.

Gun in hand, he reached out and flicked the light switch. He moved across the wide tastefully furnished living room, his foot-steps as quiet as the house on the deep pile rug. He went from room to room, snapping on lights, searching for Kate.

He didn't find her. But in Kate's sweet-smelling bedroom the tubes of the polished hi-fi set beside the head of her Hollywood bed were fairly warm. Kate or somebody else had been here recently.

Back in the living room he flipped pages of the phone book till he found the number of Arky Calahan's penthouse apartment, then sat down and dialed. In the deep quiet of the house his breathing was loud and harsh.

Calahan himself answered the phone. "Yes? Who is

it?"

By the gruff sound of his voice Tabor knew Calahan had a cigar stuck in the middle of his flat face.

"This is Tank."

There was a short pause and then Calahan spoke up, saying, "I expected to hear from you but not this soon. Get news fast, don't you, Tank?" He sounded highly pleased with himself.

"What the hell you plan to do with Kate?"

"Nothing, if you go to the nearest police station and turn yourself in."

"Got you crapping in your drawers, eh? You don't know when I might draw a bead on your fat head."

"To me you're just a punk, Tank. It's just that you're bad for my business that I want you out of my way. Your silly doings draw too much attention to me."

"Suppose I can't see myself doing what you want?"

"If you're going to act like a fool, I'll just have to have my boys send Kate back to you, is all." Arky Calahan paused, then added flatly, "Piece by piece."

A muscle in Tabor's face twitched violently, but somehow he managed to keep his voice steady as he said what Calahan wanted to hear, the only answer that would maybe get him a little time.

"I'll need a few hours to get my business straight."

"You got two."

"I'll need more time than that. I got to sell my car and everything. If I have to live the rest of my life in prison, I'm going to do it royally."

There was a lot of silence on the other end of the line, then, finally, Calahan said shortly: "All right, Tank, you got more time. But at the latest, I want to hear of your surrender to the police on the six-forty-five news. That's every second of time you'll get. Got that?"

Tabor told him he had it, then said: "Only I do no

cooperating unless I talk to Kate at sixty-thirty this evening. I want to be sure she's still with us."

"Give me a phone number and I'll have her call you," Calahan said in a smooth buddy-buddy voice.

Tabor grinned tightly at the mouthpiece of the phone. The bastard, he thought. Giving Arky your phone number would be begging him to send a flock of his hoods to your house. In less than ten minutes after he asked his puppets down at police headquarters for the information, Arky would know the location of the building wrapped around the phone.

"No. I'll call you," Tabor said. "Just have her where I can talk to her. And, Arky, I don't want Kate mistreated in any way. I'll be able to tell by her voice and if she's been roughed up, I don't turn myself in. Instead I'll go on a hunt for anybody who works for you. Not just for Trigger Slim and Croaker and Moe. But anybody on your pay-roll—your dope dealers, pickup men, bartenders, lawyers. Everybody. When I catch up with one I'll put a bullet in his brain. I'll probably toss a couple of homemade bombs at you too." He chuckled, a dry laugh without a sign of cheer in it. "Sure, the cops or your boys would eventually get me. But before they do, I'll have your help afraid to do your work. That would just about wreck your setup, wouldn't it, Arky?"

With that question he lowered the receiver to its berth, sure that Calahan had got the message.

For a minute he stood there knuckling his chin, thinking. Turning himself in to the law wouldn't help Kate, he knew. It would only get her murdered. Arky Calahan couldn't chance having anybody with guts enough to have him dragged into court on a snatch beef running loose. Kate had that kind of nerve.

But maybe that talk to Calahan about wanting to speak to Kate at six-thirty this evening would keep her unharmed till then. Another thought jolted home and Tabor picked up the phone again and dialed. If he managed to take Kate from Calahan, he'd feel better if Ruthie, Bill's wife, and the kids were someplace far away. Arky would surely think of snatching them next, to try to pressure him into returning to the pokey.

Half an hour later Tabor was letting himself into Jock's apartment. Jock was standing in front of the big chair slow-tapping the palm of his left hand with a rolled-up newspaper. Tabor closed the door and leaned his back against it, his hands gripping the knob. By the troubled expression on Jock's face he knew the big guy had got the news about Kate. His own face must have shown the bad news too.

Jock said: "You already know about Arky kidnaping Kate Lamain, don't you?"

Tabor nodded. "How can I tip up on him in his penthouse?"

Jock gave him a slow headshake. "There's only one way up. The elevator. When you get on it you might as well be in a television studio." He tilted his Leghorn to the back of his head with the newspaper, then explained, "Arky's got the elevator gimmicked so he can see anybody in it on a screen in his apartment from the time it starts up."

Tabor got up off the door and began to prowl the room with his hands shoved deep into his pants pocket. Jock sat down in the big chair, draped a leg over the arm of it and watched him. A moment later Tess came from the bedroom tying the sash of her robe. Tabor stopped in front of her. Her eyes were wide, searching his face, and he knew she'd heard what Jock said about Kate.

Over Tess's head he looked across to where Jock was sitting. Jock's face was sad.

"Albino got a phone?" Tabor asked.

"Under Rose's name. Harris."

Tabor moved across the floor. At the phone he sat down and leafed through the thick telephone directory. Before six-forty-five this evening they had to find out where Arky Calahan was holding Kate. He found the brunette's number and fingered the dial.

The phone on the other side of town shrilled several times; he waited. Along the sides of the drawn window shades he could see the sky. It looked gray and friendless, but the breeze coming in through the screen was cool and refreshing. After what seemed like a long time to him, Rose's slurry voice came through the receiver. "Hullo?"

"Girlfriend, this is Tank. Heard anything about a girl named Kate Lamain being snatched by some of Calahan's gunsels? Trigger Slim's one of them. And I imagine, Moe."

"Uh-uh. Friend of yours?"

He told her yes and asked her if Albino had come in. She made a nasty sound.

"That bastard only comes here to collect."

"Any idea where he is?"

"Someplace chippie-chasing. Where else? Only he's probably caught up with a piece of that penitentiary pork by now, since the bars are closed. Probably is somewhere shacked up. But I don't know where."

He felt his chances slipping. His main hope had been Albino. Since the Albino had known Calahan had sent some of his boys after Kate, Tabor reasoned the guy also probably knew where they were holding her.

"All right, girlfriend. If you find out where your old man is or where Trigger Slim and his pals are holding Kate, buzz me."

"Will do. How much time you got?"

"Until six-forty-five this evening."

There was a pause on the other end. Tabor looked

across the room. Tess and Jock were watching him, their faces, a little drawn, showing their concern.

"Tank," Rose said, "that ain't much time in a deal like this. You gotta move an' move fast. So I tell you what. Since I can get about more freely, you lay dead for a while. I'm gonna get dressed an' get out on the track. Might pick up a word or two. I found out about you, but I know you didn't bump your brother. Some more of Arky's doings, eh?"

"Yeah," he said. "Look, girlfriend, I may not be able to stick around here, so if you get a lead and call and I'm not here, beat it back home. I'll make it a point to call you every half hour. And thanks, girlfriend."

"Okay, but no thanks to me. I'm just trying to rate this ticket you gave me to anywhere. See you."

After breaking the connection, Tabor began calling the joints, whorehouses, every place he knew of that was open. He talked to doctors, lawyers, boosters, cannons, bookies, torpedoes, con men, winos, pimps, junkies, whores, jasper broads, and a dozen or more queenies. When he put the phone down the sun was out, bright and hot. And he still had no idea where to begin to look to find either Albino or Kate.

Everybody he'd talked to had given him the same story. "Sorry, old dude, but I haven't heard a word." Or something similar. And when he mentioned that it was some of Arky Calahan's hooligans who had Kate, they hurriedly claimed to have heard even less.

Now, several hours later, Tabor sat slumped in the deep chair, staring blankly at the floor and absently sipping at a cup of the strong black coffee Tess had brewed for them. His eyes stung and fatigue had his body feeling as if it were coated with lead. Jock was at the phone trying his luck, but so far, like Tabor, he hadn't even got a murmur of news of Albino's whereabouts.

THE DEADLY PAY-OFF

Tabor silently cursed their luck. He wished Steve Novack were in town. The old ex-racket boss would know something. Only Steve wouldn't be back in Milwaukee until sometime tonight.

Frowning, he looked up as Tess came from the kitchen, carrying the newspaper Jock had brought in this morning in one hand and a plate of sandwiches in the other. After taking Jock a sandwich, she came over and sat on the arm of Tabor's chair.

"Here, eat." She held the plate of sandwiches out to him. Then her voice became edged with anger. "Did you read the tale they got in the paper about you and Bill?"

He waved aside the sandwiches and took the newspaper. The story, along with pictures of him and Bill, was on the front page. Right under Tabor's mug shot were the words *Mad-Dog Killer*. Directly below their names was the story:

A private detective was shot to death yesterday in his brother's fashionable West Street hotel apartment.

The victim was William Tabor, 29, of West Allis. He was shot twice in the neck and twice in the chest with a .45 revolver. Police are looking for the victim's brother, Tank Tabor, 33, internationally known gambler, in connection with the killing. Several witnesses told police they heard the shots and saw the brother leave his apartment shortly afterward.

An examination showed that the victim had been brutally beaten before he was murdered. Dr. Paul Heletz, county medical examiner, who performed the post mortem on the body came up with this report:

Crushing injuries to left thorax with multiple rib fractures. Fractured pelvis.

That was more of Monkey Face Moe's work. Tabor's

fist clenched on the paper. One day soon that muscle mouthed son-of-a-bitch was going to do a lot of dying. He took a sip of coffee, read on.

Two officers of the vice squad saw the older Tabor leaving his hotel a few minutes after his brother was killed. In response to a tip that the suspect had purchased a supply of narcotics, Detectives Joseph Damratowski and Walter Shepanek arrived on the scene just as the suspect was getting into his car. When Tabor saw the detectives, he left his car and was the winner of a foot race with Detective Shepanek.

A search of the gambler's apartment by the detectives turned up a cache of uncut heroin, valued at $10,000. The detectives believe the gambler is the supplier for a gang of teen-age dope peddlers who in recent months have been preying on other high school kids, turning them into users. The day before, Tabor had been arrested for forcing a sixteen-year-old girl to use cocaine and also for two charges of armed robbery and one of assault with intent to kill. He is out on a $50,000 cash bail. Under further questioning last night by Detective Shepanek, the girl said she had asked the suspect's brother, the slain private eye, to stop the elder Tabor from selling dope to school kids.

It is the opinion of the public that the private eye was beaten, then killed by his brother when he confronted him with what the girl had told him.

They were damned generous with their opinions, Tabor thought.

Scowling, he gave the paper back to Tess and got a sandwich off the plate on her lap.

She said angrily: "Where in the world did they get it?"

Jock answered her question.

"From Arky Calahan." The big guy had given the phone a rest and was chain-lighting a cigarette. He blew out some smoke, then explained the thing to her. "The cops found the dope in Tank's apartment all right. You can bet on that and have yourself a cinch win. Arky saw to that, and when Goaldie fed the cops that story, she was giving out with what Arky had told her to say. It's nasty but neat."

"But how can he get away with it?" Tess said. "After all—"

That's when the phone jangled.

Jock snatched up the receiver, identified himself, listened a moment, then jerked his head for Tabor to get over there. "Rose." He trotted across the room and grabbed the phone from Jock.

"Hello, hello."

"Tank," the slur was missing from Rose's voice. It was fast with excitement, "I located Kate Lamain. You gotta hurry though; they're going to get rid of her sometime this afternoon, I heard. They got her at Trigger Slim's place. Out on the hill. Couldn't get the address. Tank, from what I hear, that's what Arky ordered them to do. To do Kate in, I mean. And Trigger Slim talked Moe and Croaker into holding up on the order for a while so he could use Kate as a lever to squeeze some money out of Tess Andrews, Ritchie's wife."

Covering the mouthpiece, he looked down at Jock. "Know where Trigger Slim lives?"

"Out on the hill."

Tabor gave the brunette a hasty but warm word of thanks and cradled the receiver.

"Tess, get your money. This place will be too hot for us afterwards." Trigger Slim's greed for the geets might turn out to be the best thing in the world for Kate—if they could get to Slim's place in time.

Chapter Sixteen

On the hill was Harlem, Little Italy and Chicago's Maxwell Street all in one. Trigger Slim lived in the heart of it, in a sinful-looking six-flat frame building that stood in the middle of a block choked with booze joints, greasy spoons, dingy second-hand clothing stores and pushcarts of all sizes filled with everything from cabbage sprouts to frozen custards.

They crawled on past Trigger Slim's building. He saw they weren't going to find a place to park in the block. Trucks, cars, and carts had every inch of both curbs covered. He told Jock to try the alley.

When they got around in back, Jock parked the Roadmaster close to the front of a sagging three-car garage behind Slim's building. The stench of the garbage-heavy alley made Tabor's stomach queasy. He lit a cigarette. The smoke helped some, but not much.

Tess eased the Continental up behind them, and he got out, narrowing his eyelids against the torture of the two o'clock sun, and walked back to her. He leaned his elbows on the window sill. In the strong sunlight the strain in her beautiful face showed up more clearly. The skin was tight across her slightly raised cheekbones. But even though she was frightened, he saw her chin was still firm.

"If you hear shooting and we're not back ten minutes later, go tell the District Attorney the story. No cops. Nobody but the D. A."

Tess nodded. She started to say something, but he covered her mouth with his. Her full lips, as always, were soft and fresh. When he let her go he walked away and didn't look back. He didn't want to see the pain in her eyes.

He stopped beside the Roadmaster and looked up at Trigger Slim's third-floor flat. A wide, unscreened porch extended from one side of the building to the other. The windows of the apartment were shaded and some of the slanting rays of the sun made them look as though they were on fire. He stood there dragging thoughtfully on his cigarette, wondering how to go about crashing the place. Then he let the cigarette fall to the ground, mashed it underfoot, and turned around to the car.

"What do you say, Jock?" How do we go about getting in?"

Jock thumbed the Leghorn to the back of his head. "Blitz the joint is all I can see. Go up on the porch and kick in the window." The big guy sounded like he was discussing a minor league baseball game. "The joint's got three outs—front, back, and the fire escape on the side. We can't cover all of 'em."

He checked his Luger, then got out of the car. Tabor led the way through the meager gangway into a broad garbage-filled backyard. In the building to the right of them a hen leaning from a fourth-floor window was telling a chick on the floor below what she'd do if she had been the one to find some strange lipstick on her old man's shorts.

"... and, honey chile, then I'd wait for the bastard to go to sleep and see how much scalding-hot lye water he could guzzle. That's just what I'd do, me, if I was you. Why the dirty no good ..."

Jock chuckled. "A lesson in home economics."

When they got upstairs on Trigger Slim's porch Tabor put his ear against the jamb of the closed door. Music was playing and somebody was guffawing. As he listened the music came to a stop. The raucous laughter continued. He tried the door knob. Locked.

For a brief moment he was tempted to blast the lock to hell, but decided not to. There was no way of telling whom he might hit.

Fisting his gun, he moved over to the window. Sweat had soaked his underclothes and shirt. He raised his foot half aware that the dames next door had stopped running off at the jib and were eyeballing them. He rammed his foot against the windowpane. One of the dames tried to bust a gut hollering. He knew if they didn't get things over with and get out fast, they'd have half the cops in Milwaukee crawling over them.

Glass was still tinkling down on the window sill when he dived through the window. The shade came down around his head and for a moment he scuffled around on the floor getting it off. He got the thing from over his head just as footsteps pounded into the room. When he twisted around, still on the floor, Calahan's watchdog, Croaker, was in the doorway with a gun in his hand.

Before Tabor could bring up his gun Croaker fired and he felt lead scorch his left shoulder, feeling like red-hot pliers ripping a plug out of his skin. The shot knocked him over, sideways. He rolled frantically, desperately, and came up beside an icebox. He scooted around. He'd got to his knees when another slug burned across his scalp.

Everything went blurry, as if he were looking through a piece of cracked isinglass. He was on his hands and knees, shaking his head. He told himself to lift his gun and squeeze the trigger. He couldn't make it. He knelt there, swaying, watching Croaker move farther into the kitchen to get a clean shot at him.

The guy never got it, because Jock, a strained grin splitting his lips, was climbing in the window, climbing in choking the trigger of his deadly looking Luger. The gun blasted three times and right in Croaker's face. The hood's gun roared into the ceiling. He rocked backward and spun, took one plunging step and sprawled across the breakfast table.

Suddenly the apartment was quiet. Tabor got up off the floor, still wobbly in the knees, and headed for the door, thinking the punk would never rape anybody else. He skirted Croaker's outstretched legs and stepped out into a dim hall that ran the length of the building. There were three doors on either side of the hall. One near the front was open. Jock came up behind him and Tabor motioned for him to shake down the rooms on the right while he worked the left. The quietness worried him. He wondered if the rest of the gunsels had escaped, taking Kate with them.

He sleeved blood off his face and started for the first door on his side. Then he heard a door bang open, then footsteps—light, fast-moving footsteps.

He ran for the open door up front. When he made the turn at the door he came face to face with Goaldie, the little junkie chippie who had got him fouled up on that dope rap. She was at the head of the stairs, getting ready to quit the scene. For a moment she stood there, frozen, clutching a valise she carried with both skinny hands, her mouth hanging open in shocked disbelief.

"Come here, you little bitch," he growled.

But the little gal had other ideas—and a lot of rabbit in her. Disregarding the guns in his hands, she turned and scooted down the steps.

He started after her and the chippie swung around suddenly and flung her valise at his legs. Her aim was good.

When Tabor stopped tumbling he was in a corner on the second landing, twisted up like a pretzel. He lay there cursing through his teeth and trying to shake some of the fuzz out of his head. Dimly he heard footsteps coming down the stairs and then he was painfully aware of Jock helping him up.

"Tank, you all right, man?"

"Guess so." He tried his legs, feeling a little foolish for having let Goaldie trick him. The big guy didn't ask him what had happened and he wasn't thinking about telling him. Except for a few more bruises here and there and a headache with a bass beat, he was okay.

Jock was saying, "Kate's in the back room. She's alive, but they must've doped her up because she's out."

At least she was alive. Suddenly Tabor felt as if a great pressure had been lifted from his back. He stooped to get his gun and saw that Goaldie's valise lay open at the foot of the stairs. On top were some pink silk underclothes, badly in need of laundering, and several white envelopes with the chippie's name on them in red ink. He told Jock to bring the valise. Then he ran back up the stairs, surprised that he'd fallen so far and hadn't broken any bones.

Kate lay on a long throw rug on her back, beside a wide rumpled bed, one arm bent like a sign bearer's, the other hidden beneath the folds of the faded pink spread hanging half off the bed. She looked as if she were in a peaceful sleep, her breathing soft and even, her beautiful features relaxed.

She was fully dressed. The hoods had been getting ready to move her, Tabor thought, as he knelt beside her. They'd probably dropped her in their haste to get away. He gathered Kate in his arms, thinking if he and Jock had been five minutes longer getting there, they'd have been busting into an empty apartment.

The girl Rose came to his mind as he straightened up with Kate and moved out of the room. The brunette had earned the fifteen hundred bucks he'd given her a million times over.

He walked down the stairs with Jock at his heels. There were scores of people hanging out of the windows of the buildings along the alley now. They stared at them in silence. Tabor was glad of that. He didn't want trouble with them. From the way his head and shoulder felt he knew he couldn't handle much more trouble. Every step he took fogged his eyes and he could feel the blood from the wound in his shoulder sliming his whole left side.

When they got downstairs, Tess was coming through the gangway. She saw them and stopped, lowering the gun in her hand to her side.

"She's alive," Tabor told her, answering the question in her eyes. "But I want a doctor to look at her."

"I know a guy," Jock said. "We can go to his house from here. He won't talk and he lives by himself."

Chapter Seventeen

The doctor Jock knew was reluctant at first to doctor on them and not report the matter to the police. But Jock had melted his reluctance with a short talk and a long one-hundred-dollar bill.

While the doctor bandaged his shoulder, Tabor sat in a kitchen chair, sipping some of his good brandy. The doc was pretty old, maybe seventy-five or eighty, but his hands felt steady and sure.

Tabor asked him again: "You sure the girl's going to be all right?"

"Oh, sit still and quit worrying," the doctor told him, pressing a strip of adhesive tape in place. "You're worse off than that girl. The drug will wear off in a few hours and she'll be fine after some hot soup and a bit of rest. But you, young man, are going to fall flat on your face if you don't get some sleep soon."

How right you are, doc, he thought. Fatigue had every nerve in his body twanging. He touched up his brandy, idly wondering how long could he go without sleep on an alcoholic diet. Not long, he guessed. The stuff hadn't been brewed to make you sleep-resistant, but to petrify you. Tossing off the rest of the brandy, he set the glass on the sparkling white porcelain table beside him and then offered the doctor a proposition.

"Another hundred bucks, doc, if you let us stay here and keep mum about it. Say, for a day or so."

The old boy sighed. "Money, money. The root of all evil," he said. "How true. How true." When he finished taping the bandage together, he held out his hand to Tabor, grinning. "Ah, make me evil, son."

"Doc, you're a businessman."

He gave the old doctor another bill. The doctor folded it, inclining his head in the direction of the living room.

"There are four rooms upstairs. Use any of them. Bath's at the end of the hall. You'll find towels in the rooms."

They went out into the living room. It was enormous and filled with antiquated but spotlessly clean brown leather furniture. Tabor didn't see the big guy and he looked at Tess sitting curled up in one of the big chairs with a magazine on her lap.

"Where'd Jock go?"

"To his apartment to try to get some of our clothes."

The doctor told them, "You folks go on up to bed. Both of you need sleep. I'll look after the other girl."

"Thanks, doc. And wake me when she comes out of it."

Forty-five minutes later, after washing his battered body as well as he could, Tabor was tucked between the crisp white sheets on one of the doctor's feathermattressed beds. The shade was drawn and the spacious room was quiet and pleasant. He was hashing over the charges against him in his mind. Mostly wondering how the hell was he going to get out from under them.

Somewhere there were flaws in Arky Calahan's frames, loose ends, he knew. There had to be. No crooked caper was ever perfect. But for the life of him, his brains couldn't pick out a single bit of evidence in his favor.

Yes, Calahan had viced him. Had viced the hell out of him.

His door opened and Tess came into the room. "Almost asleep?" she said.

"Just thinking."

She sat on the bed beside him, her slender hands folded in her lap.

"Tank, what are you going to do now?"

"About Calahan?"

She nodded.

"Right now," he told her, "my idea bank on that subject is exhausted. All I can do is hope Kate's got something for me. Jock said Calahan's boys love to try to gas each other with what they've done."

"You think they talked in front of Kate?"

"Maybe. They had no reason not to. They didn't intend for Kate to walk away from them."

Tess winced and was quiet for a time, looking down into his eyes. Then she said in a low voice: "It isn't pity for me, is it, Tank? I mean the way you've changed toward me since—since what happened to me last night."

Unmindful of his sore spots, he pulled her down to him. Pity for her could never have brought out of him what his love for her brought out in his kiss. He knew she felt it, too. Her soft lips opened under his and her fingers bit into his arms as he tried to eat her up. She was delicious. When the kiss was over, her eyes had a glazed look in them.

Tabor waited a few seconds until his head stopped swimming and his breathing slowed down some. Then he said: "I've never stopped loving you."

She slipped her hand into his, looking deep into his eyes again. "Then we've never stopped loving each other," she said, and the soft richness he loved so much to hear was in her voice.

He squeezed her hand, hoping all this would be over soon so he could settle down with her and begin to live. From the way he felt now, he realized he hadn't been living for the past four years.

Tess was saying, "I know how that must sound. My telling you I've never stopped loving you. But it's true. Ritchie knew it when he married me. I told him. Guess I married him because he loved me and said it didn't matter how I felt about you." She drew in a deep breath and the front of the dress fascinated him, caused his breath to catch in his throat. "But, Tank, I waited eighteen months, after they told me you were dead."

He sat straight up in the bed. "After who told you what?"

Tess seemed startled. "The War Department sent me a letter telling me you were killed in action. At first I refused to believe it. Couldn't believe it. But your letters stopped coming." She lifted her shoulders slightly and let them fall again.

"Then you were already married to Ritchie when I came back and busted in on you two in bed?"

"Of course. We'd been married—" She broke off, her face turning rosy red. "You didn't think—you thought I was cheating on you? Oh, Tank, how could you?" Her eyes were hurt.

"But, honey, I didn't know."

"You didn't know you'd been listed as dead?"

He shook his head. "Not by the War Department, I didn't. Of course when I got back from overseas, a couple of the fellows said they'd heard I'd got it. But I put it down as wishful thinking."

"But your letters. Why did you stop writing to me?"

"Honey, I didn't get to do any writing in the Jap prison camp I was in. It was just a small Northern Burma outpost and those boys had never heard of the Red Cross. If they had, the GI's around there sure as hell didn't know it. Only time we saw any paper was when they put a notice or something on the bulletin board."

When he'd finished talking, there were tears in Tess's eyes. "Tank, I'm sorry."

"It's over now."

She fascinated him some more by inhaling deeply again.

"God," she whispered, leaning her forehead on his chest, "I do hope Kate heard something we can use to get Arky off our necks, so we can go home." She kissed his chest. "I want you alone."

"For how long?"

"For a lifetime, silly, of course." She giggled. "We have a lot of making up to do, don't you think?"

The way she was fascinating him he wanted to start making up right then and there. But he controlled the urge. It wouldn't be decent he thought, to try to touch her after what she'd been through last night.

"We'll pull out of this," he said, and hoped he was right. "We'll have that lifetime together to make up."

At a few minutes past eleven that night, after taking advantage of the sirloin dinner Tess prepared for them, Tabor sat on the high leather davenport in the doctor's enormous living room, listening to Kate tell what she had heard while being held by Arky Calahan's mob. The sleep, plus the tasty hot meal, had him feeling almost A-one again. Most of the ache had gone out of his head and his shoulder wasn't too bad. Just stiff and a bit itchy. He was dressed in another of Jock's neatly cut summer suits, a cocoa-brown flannel that felt like a feather on him.

So far Kate hadn't given them anything they could use to hammer Calahan out of existence with. Most of what she'd told them Tabor had already guessed, the part about Arky Calahan wanting all of them out of the way—permanently. He was thankful for one thing. Those punks hadn't hurt Kate in any way. Kate said that Trigger Slim and Croaker had started to treat her like they'd done Tess, but she told them she was diseased and they changed their minds.

Kate was saying, "They talked about that newspaper reporter who got killed a few months ago. That's what they talked about mostly." She hesitated, looking around at Tess who sat on the other side of her on the davenport. "You know about your husband?"

"That he wasn't what I thought him to be?" Tess nodded, her face showing nothing of the sickness she must have felt. "I know."

"Well," Kate went on, "from some things Trigger Slim said this morning, I gathered that Ritchie had something to do with killing that reporter."

At that Jock stopped rummaging through the valise Goaldie had upset Tabor with this afternoon and looked up. "The reporter that was shot-gunned out on Highway 41 six months ago?" he asked, draping one long leg over the arm of his chair. "That the guy?"

"Yes. Slim said if Ritchie hadn't gotten himself fouled up on the job they did on the reporter, none of this would've been happening. I guess he meant the trouble we're having with Arky. That's about all I heard, except their talk about women."

Tabor lit a cigarette and absently rolled the dead match stem between his fingers. Something was buzzing around in his head, something Jock had told him in the pokey. He looked down the room at the big guy.

"Say the cops figured Steve Novack could tell them something about the reporter's death, if he wanted to?"

Jock nodded. Tabor dropped the match stick in the glass ashtray on the coffee table in front of the davenport, stubbed out his partially smoked cigarette and then got to his feet.

"Think I'll drop in on him. He should be back in the city by now." When Jock started to get up, he shook his head. "Stick here with the girls. If I get anything I can't follow through on alone, I'll call you. What's the phone number here, anyway?"

Tabor repeated the number to himself several times and then remembered to ask whether there was anything in Goaldie's valise.

"Not much. Some underclothes and four empty envelopes, three with nothing but her name on 'em, and one with 'Call Nina at two' on it. Who Nina is I don't know."

"That makes two of us," Tabor told him.

Tess stood up, thoughtful a moment. "Nina ... Ritchie used to get phone calls from a woman named Nina. I never bothered to find out who she was. She used to call at least once a week. Sometimes two and three times."

"Probably one of the gals hangs out at Arky's bar." Tabor looked down at Kate. "Tomorrow sometime, you're going to contact the D. A. and swear out warrants for Calahan and his boys for kidnap."

"Whatever you say. Would that help you all?"

"Maybe." They'd heard over the radio that two first-degree murder warrants had been issued for him and Tess and Jock for the deaths of Slade and Croaker, and that a forty-state alarm was out on them. The net was drawing tighter and tighter. "A kidnap charge," he explained, "might take Calahan off our back for a day or two and give us a chance to get in a few good licks. Of course I'm assuming the D. A.'s not on Calahan's payroll and will issue warrants for him and his boys. We'll see. I got to beat it now."

For a moment Kate continued to look up at him, trying hard to hide the concern in her eyes, but not quite making it. Then, not looking at him, she told him gruffly: "You be careful, you big baboon. And don't think I've forgotten that crack you made about me helping Arky frame you. I oughtta bust you one."

"You should, you really should. I wouldn't even duck." He leaned down to kiss her, but she turned her face away.

"Darn it, Tank, go on." Her voice was a broken sob. "Don't break me up."

He turned and moved toward the door. Tess walked with him.

"Kate loves you, Tank," she said. "I don't blame her," she whispered, and pulled his head down. "I don't blame her at all," she said again, breathing warm sweet breath into his mouth.

Chapter Eighteen

It was twelve-twenty when Tabor curbed the Continental in front of Steve Novack's saloon. It seemed he was dripping water out of every pore in his body.

Steve's joint was jammed between a girlie show and a barbecue house. The barbecue house had the immediate area smelling like smoked ribs. Tabor got out and ambled across the broad walk, glancing at the life-sized pictures in front of the girlie show. All of the babes had a lot of everything and most of it was spilling out of bikinis and bras that didn't have enough material in them to make a midget a pocket handkerchief.

In the dim saloon, nickel-and-dime gamblers, fading hookers, and aged mackmen had all of the stools at the long bar covered, so he settled for one of the few vacant booths. He lit a cigarette and then wagged a finger at the wide-bottomed waitress.

When she wiggled over to him, he asked her, "Steve around?"

"Busy out back. Drinking anything?"

He shook his head, gave her a half-a-buck. "Tell Steve Tank wants to see him."

His name hit her. "Tank, Tank." She wrinkled her forehead, thinking. "I've heard that name somewhere. You know me?"

He grinned up at her, hoping it looked good. It felt sickly. She had probably heard his name over the radio, on the news flashes or police broadcasts. "Uh-uh," he said. "But we can work on that later if it's all right with you. Right now I have some business with Steve."

The babe left. But her forehead was still wrinkled. She was digging in her memory box so hard she was forgetting to put that extra wiggle in her walk.

He watched her disappear through a scarlet-curtained doorway at the back of the room. Then he put out his half-smoked cigarette and leaned against the back of the booth. Somebody played the jukebox and the music, along with the smoke and the babble of voices in the place, made his head ache. His thoughts went across town to where Jock and Kate and Tess were hiding.

Tabor looked up and saw Steve coming toward him, nodding and smiling at his customers as he passed. When the old ex-racket boss got to the booth his bushy-browed eyes deserted his smile, letting the lower part of his tough lined face carry it alone.

"You careless, Tank," he murmured. "Letting these bums get a look at you. Come in my office."

Steve didn't wait for him to say anything, but turned abruptly and walked away.

Tabor slid out of the booth and sidled between the crowded tables, through the gabble and alcohol laughter and canned music, and the smell of peanuts and beer and sweaty flesh. The waitress was standing over by the bar looking at him, her lower lip tucked between her teeth. He knew she was still trying to remember where she'd heard his name. When he came abreast of her he paused. "I'll be around when you get off," he lied. The girl didn't answer, just kept staring at him, her forehead ridged.

He trailed Steve through the curtained doorway at the back of the room, up three steps, and into his large air-cooled office. Steve pushed the thick wooden door together and motioned to a chair, "You damn careless, Tank," he said again, as he went behind the green metal desk and dropped his squatty frame into a swivel chair.

Tabor said, "The waitress told me you were busy."

Steve slapped that down with a wave of his hand. "No excuse. You know I'm never too busy to see you." He shoved aside some green ledgers and tablets on his desk and leaned forward, looking at him and shaking his head slowly. "I no understand you no more, Tank." He tapped the side of his head with an index finger. "You got brains. Plenty good brains. That is why I no understand why you sit out front and let those hungry bastards get a good look at you. Some of them read the newspapers, too. And crazy as the cops are to get you, any one of those bastards out there could think of a way to parlay you into a hundred dollars. If he couldn't get a hundred, he would sell you for fifty. Twenty, ten—anything he could get."

"I don't think anyone out there recognized me." He hoped the waitress hadn't placed him.

Steve took a bottle of Scotch, seltzer water, and a couple of paper cups from one of the lower desk drawers. He poured up, reached Tabor a cup, and leaned back in his swivel chair. "What's on your mind, Tank?" he asked, after touching up his drink.

Tabor sat on the edge of the chair, with his forearms resting on his knees. He looked straight into Steve's bushy-browed eyes. "Know who knocked off that newspaper reporter?"

Steve's face smoothed into blank stupidity.

A minute ticked by. Out in the bar the fast-lifers had got louder. Without looking away from Steve's tough old face, Tabor unfastened his collar and let the cool air from the portable air conditioner on the window sill blow inside his shirt. The faint scent of barbecue coming from the joint next door smelled good. He knew Steve knew something about the reporter's death, maybe not who had done the killing. But something. His question had rocked the old guy pretty hard.

Another minute ticked off into nowhere.

Then Steve drained his cup, crumpled it, and lobbed it into a green wire basket in the corner behind him. Fingering his gold watch chain, he looked at Tabor as if Tabor had asked his advice on how to kill his best pal so he could crawl in bed with his wife. "I know nothing about the newspaperman," he said flatly. "Nothing."

"Nothing, Steve?" he asked quietly.

Steve took a silver case from the breast pocket of his coat, pressed a button on the side of it with a big-knuckled thumb, and a cork-tipped cigarette popped up. He looked at him and Tabor shook his head. Steve lit the cigarette with the lighter built in the case and said: "This is a big question, Tank, to ask even me, your friend."

"I've got a big reason for asking it. It's not myself I'm worried about too much—you know that without my telling you. It's Tess and Kate and Jock Adams I'm thinking of. I've got to get them clean, got to get Tess and Jock from under two murder raps and Kate from under Calahan's hammer. So you can see why I'm knocking on any door trying to get something on Calahan and his boys. Do you help me?"

"Help you? How? I know nothing—nothing, absolutely. Some money you can have if you want." Steve put his cigarette case back into his coat and pulled a billfold from his hip pocket that looked like an undersized balloon tire. "Five thousand? Ten? You name it." His thumb passed back and forth over the top of the billfold, riffling the bills in it. "How much?"

"Put your bread away, Steve," Tabor said. "If I don't find out what I believe is true, bread won't do me much good. I'm not sure, but I think Calahan had something to do with knocking off the guy. You coming in with some news?"

"Why you think so? You know something maybe, huh?"

He gave it to him straight. "I'm pretty sure you've heard about Calahan snatching Kate by now, so I won't go into that. While they had her, she heard Trigger Slim leaking at the lips about them hitting the reporter. Ritchie Andrews was in on it. What I'm trying to do is dig up evidence that'll tie Bill's and Ritchie's and the reporter's killings in one big bundle and throw it at Calahan in a way that he can't duck it. If I can do that, he or one of his mob might cop out to get some of the weight up off himself and tell the truth about everything. That's the only possible out I can see."

He poured the rest of the Scotch down his throat and set the paper cup beside his chair. Then he brought his attention back to Steve and waited. The ex-racket boss puffed on his cigarette and continued to stare at him, saying nothing.

After a time Tabor said: "Of course you know Calahan's behind every bit of this."

"The grapevine, she's been working." Steve frowned. "This Tess and Jock I don't know, but I don't like to see you and Kate mixing with Arky. He's a heartless son-of-a-bitch—respects nobody's rights. Now he's trying to get all the nice kids like him. He's flooding the city with dope and pretty soon what have we got? A town full of lightweight Arky Calahans, scratching, slobbering junkie kids who is respecting nobody's rights, either." He made a hopeless gesture.

"Well, do you talk about the newspaper guy or not? That might wreck Arky."

Steve put away his billfold, dropped his cigarette into an ash stand beside the desk, and stood up. His face looked as if he'd just been sentenced to die and had been appointed his own executioner. He went to the window and looked out into the alley, his hands folded in back of him. Tabor raked his thumbnail across a match and lit a cigarette. He smoked and waited, giving Steve a chance to make up his mind.

After what seemed like a long time Steve faced around again. He looked at Tabor and shook his head.

"Tank, I know nothing."

Tabor asked quietly, "Know who you're lying to now, Steve?"

The ex-racket boss winced noticeably but held his silence.

"This is me ... Tank," he reminded Steve in the same quiet tone. "The chump who gave you twenty grand to get on your feet again when the combine bounced you out of the organization with nothing but the suit you had on your back. The chump who ran interference for you when some of your old mob wanted to do you in." He got up, went to the door. Hand on knob, he looked back. Steve hadn't moved. He stood there wincing as if Tabor had hit him. Tabor went on. "Yeah, I said chump. Because I can see now that that's what I was for thinking you were worth helping. You're—"

"Okay, okay, okay!" Steve all but shouted the words. His old face was twisted with anger and fear.

Tabor felt excitement tingling in his chest.

Steve tried to get another cigarette going, but he had to give it up. His hand shook so badly he couldn't find the end of the cigarette with the flame. He threw the gold case among the ledgers and tablets on the desk. Then, he flopped into his chair, got another paper cup, poured himself a second drink, a tall one, and flung it down his throat. "You want I should get killed?" he gasped. He put the empty cup on the desk, glaring across the room at him. "You want this to happen to me?"

Tabor said, "You know better than that, Steve."

"I know nothing, anyway. Rumors, rumors. This all I hear. Only you know, like me, repeating rumors can get you killed as good as anything."

Tabor crossed the room to the desk and looked down at Steve's troubled face. He hated to push the old guy but here was Tess and Jock and Kate to think about.

He had to take Calahan out for them. For himself too. "What're the rumors?"

Steve breathed out a lot of air, lifted his arms, and let them fall back to the arms of the chair. "It's about a dame. Nina Massey, she name." He paused, shook his head. "I no guarantee this is pure. Like I say, I'm only telling you rumors.

"Well, this Nina Massey, I hear she's got something on somebody. Something that make it worthwhile for that somebody to put her up in a penthouse on Lake Drive, a four hundred a month layout, and buy her Cadillacs." Steve held up two fingers. "This many."

Tabor sat down again. "How does that connect her with the murdered reporter?"

"I don't know. I just give you what I hear. Only before the guy came up dead, this Nina she's bumming drinks from joint to joint. After the guy got hit, three days after, this same Nina gets this penthouse, starts changing Cadillacs twice a day, and passing out twenty-dollar tips to every waiter in every joint she goes in."

Tabor nodded. "She still doing it?"

"Faster than ever." Steve shook his head. "Nobody knows where she gets all this money. She no talk. But everybody knows she got it right after this news guy got himself killed, and everybody is wondering."

"Anyone ever try making her give out with some news about where she's getting the greenies?"

Steve held up three fingers. "Three guys she fool with before going bigtime. They try to squeeze the news out of her one night last week. Next day they came up missing. Nobody seen them since. Then, just two days ago, another of her old jockeys gets burned up because she no let him ride no more and start spouting off that he's got an idea where Nina is getting the moola. A couple of hours later I hear the police found him in some vacant lot, his neck broken in these many different places." Steve showed him four fingers this time.

"What about the cops? They should be curious about her."

Steve nodded. "They were once. But somebody must have made them satisfied, because most of them call her Miss Massey now. Always before they call her something else. Nina's taxes is probably straight too. I no hear nothing about the Feds being on her high-living fanny, at least."

"That figures. Know anything else that might help me?"

Steve wasted no time in letting him know the answer was no. He shook his head in a hurry. "And tell nobody I talk with you about this Nina Massey. I am old and peaceful now and I want to die of old age."

Tabor grinned and got to his feet. "You'll never make it. Not if you still go for good whisky and fast babes like you used to. What's Nina's address?"

Steve wrote the address on a piece of paper he ripped from one of the tablets and gave it to him. "Give her no chance," he warned. "She's one foxy dame."

"We'll have a foxy good time then. I like the type." Tabor glanced at the address on the paper, then tore it into tiny pieces. "I'll go out the back way."

"Do that."

Chapter Nineteen

Tabor walked into the lavishly furnished lobby of Nina Massey's hotel-apartment building. There were three elevators operating but only the last one was at the lobby floor. He got into it and told the cute babe operator to take him all the way up. When he reached the penthouse floor he found a cool, brown-carpeted hall. Behind him the elevator's heavy doors clicked shut.

He thumbed the ivory pushbutton beside the door of Nina Massey's penthouse apartment and waited what seemed like half a minute. Then the lock snapped and the door swung in, opening on noiseless hinges.

After a fleeting glance at the pea-green rabbit perched on her left shoulder, he stared at the rest of her. The babe was worth a lot of stares. She was tall and creamy-skinned and naked, except for blue tasseled mules and a lighter blue negligee that was sheerness at its extreme. Momentarily, soft green eyes got a little wide and that was the only sign the babe showed that indicated he wasn't her best lover. She gave him plenty of time to admire the lushness of her nude body.

He didn't fake.

He goggled at it, at the full-bloom pink-tipped breasts that jutted out from her chest as if they were stuffed with cotton, at the unblemished hips that flared out lavishly and, finally, at the round, soft-looking thighs that melted into a pair of beautifully molded legs.

She laughed softly. He voice was tinged with the kind of huskiness that goes well with a dim-lit bedroom and soft, sweet music. "When you get done all I'll need is a towel."

"Didn't realize I was that obvious," Tabor said. "You Nina Massey?"

She puckered prettily, tilted her head back, and said: "I am."

If Steve had not told him, nobody could have made him believe Nina had been a joint-hopping juice head only six months ago. The gal looked like choice pickings and then some. She was it plus. He said: "I want to talk with you for a minute."

"Do you?" She shook back a head of long softly glowing red hair that hung loosely around her shoulders. Then it was her turn to give him the slow-eye business. She winked her approval. "You look even prettier than your pretty pictures."

"You know me?"

"Tank Tabor, big-time gambler, international heartbreaker of the softer sex." Nina wrinkled her nose and smiled slyly at him, with full red lips that were made to be nibbled. "See, I know it all by heart."

He grinned, relieved. Evidently she hadn't read a paper or listened to a radio in the last two days. "Now if you invite me in, we can talk about forming a Tabor fan club." She started to shake her head but before she could complete the motion, he said, "This won't take long."

"I'm expecting a visitor in a little while." She put the rabbit on the floor, then leaned through the doorway and looked in the direction of the elevator. No one was in the hall but him. "Well, if it won't take long—"

She turned back into the room and he followed her, picking up on the lazy rhythm of her lush curves as she moved to a couch and sat down. He felt himself coming alive and tightened up. He closed the door. The babe crossed her dimpled knees, completely unconcerned about his ogling at her nakedness, and waved him to a deep chair directly in front of her.

The green rabbit hopped up on the couch beside her and stretched out. Tabor looked about him. It was a gay room enclosed with three white walls and one of pink-tinted glass and decorated with low dark blue leather furniture. The glass wall, partially covered with flowing gold drapes, looked out over the glistening surface of Lake Michigan. An ankle-deep oriental rug hugged every inch of the wide floor. Near the glass wall a door flanked with panels of patterned glass stood slightly ajar and through the opening came the low sound of a tenor sax moaning "Harlem Nocturne." The musician was no tyro.

Whatever kind of game Nina-gal was playing, evidently she was playing it like a champ. It would seem that the lovely was squeezing every dram of the gravy from the golden goose.

Nina Massey said: "What can Nina do for you, pretty?"

He went back to eye-raping her. She had leaned back, bracing herself with her arms a little behind her and the palms of her hands flat on the couch. The sheer negligee lay like caressing palms across the tops of her slowly undulating breasts. He tightened up on his control some more.

"You're a trusting soul," he told her, in a husky voice.

"You're no rapo. Even if you were, though, I wouldn't put on any more clothes and wouldn't run very fast if you tried to catch me." Her smile was sly again. "You see, for years, ever since I first saw a picture of you in the paper, I've been wanting to lure you into my boudoir. You have that look that gets me. So cool and so sure of yourself. I like that."

He grunted. "I'll remember that. But right now I'd like you to explain something to me."

"Explain what, pretty?"

"About the newspaper reporter who was murdered about six months ago out on Highway 41."

Nina Massey's elbows buckled as if someone had unexpectedly walloped her in her jutting chest. She was on her elbows now. Her eyes were wide and her face had turned the color of sour buttermilk. A clothespin couldn't have pinched her nostrils much tighter than they were now. He watched the fear in the doll's eyes.

She cleared her throat a couple of times, then asked:

"What do you mean?" Her voice was chilly.

"I want you to tell me about the reporter," he said. "About his killing."

Nina stood suddenly and gave him what she thought was a smile. He gave her E for effort but the smile was about as strong as a piece of overcooked spaghetti. It slithered all over her face.

"Maybe I'd better slip on something at that," she laughed. "Our talk is going to take more time than I thought and I wouldn't want my visitor to see me like this with you. He's jealous of little ole faithful me." She swiveled it to the front of the room and floated through the door near the glass wall.

The door closed behind her with a click.

Getting to his feet, Tabor waggled an admonishing finger at the pea-green carrot-eater, then took the same route Nina gal had taken; and stood beside the door. He couldn't hear anything in there so he became a peeper.

Through the keyhole he saw his gal standing by a small wooden table dialing an ivory phone with a hand that moved with quick jerky motions. With one hand he pressed the door hard against the jamb, eased the knob around with the other. The door opened without so much as a whisper.

As he eased into Nina's bedroom and moved toward her, he was thankful that she was fond of smothering her floors with ankle-deep rugs. The gal had no idea he was on the scene until he reached around her wide hip and broke her connection.

She gave way in the knees and sagged against him; her beautiful face was looking buttermilky again. He caught her before she slid all the way to the floor. He took the receiver from her and cradled it. "No calls, baby."

Breathing fast, she snatched herself out of his arms

and wheeled around to face him. Anger was fast crowding out the fear in her green eyes. "What do you mean sneaking in here?"

"No phone calls until after we talk."

"I don't have anything to say to you!" she blazed. She whirled and ran to a triple-mirrored dresser and yanked open one of its top drawers. In three strides he was on her. He grabbed her arms.

He was none too soon.

Her hand came from the drawer gripping a pearl-handled .32 Colt. "Let me go!" she hissed, twisting furiously to get the gun aimed in his direction.

He slid his hands down her arms until they were around her wrists and forced the front of her body against the dresser. She was cursing and struggling, trying to get away. The cursing he could take. But her struggling with him, with practically nothing on, was beginning to have its effect. He felt desire come alive inside him, skittering around in his chest.

"Drop it," he commanded. He fought for control but it was a hell of a one-sided battle, with luscious Nina trying to back her soft hind parts through him. "Drop it, baby."

"Damn you!"

Their eyes met in the dresser's center mirror. She spat and glared nastily at him.

"Well, you're campaigning for it baby," he said, and ground the bones of her wrists together. Her breath caught in her throat. Slowly her fingers relaxed. The gun clattered to the dresser. "That's being a nice baby."

He pulled her away from the dresser, let go of her wrists, and immediately knew he had made a bad mistake.

Grating her teeth and hissing like an enraged cat, Nina flung herself around and clawed at his eyes with her long nails. He barely got his head out of the way in time. As it was, her nails scraped skin off his chin and snagged his shirt collar.

She screamed, "I'll ruin you!" and started at him again. She raised her leg and tried to give him the knee, low and inside, and he twisted his hip. His thigh took the blow. She thought of her long nails again and lunged at him with upraised arms.

He met her with an open-handed left hook to her chin. The impact of the blow brought her up to her toes and sent her reeling over the foot of her wide bed.

Breathing a little faster than normal, he moved up on her. The scratches on his chin where her nails had raked him stung a little. He took out his handkerchief and dabbed at the spots. The record player, a pearl gray bedside model, hadn't changed its tune. He put the handkerchief away and looked down at Nina. Desperation had made him violate every rule he'd set up for himself. What he'd done left a nasty taste in his mouth, but he couldn't turn back now, couldn't stop being a bastard, because he knew this curvaceous piece of sweet-smelling flesh was in a nasty game and had the answers to a thing or two.

"All right," he said, "let's hear your story about the reporter."

"I have nothing to tell you," she breathed. She sat up on the bed, rubbing her chin where he'd clouted her. With a couple of angry twists of her head she threw her lustrous red hair back over her shoulders. "And if you're as smart as a lot of the hustlers seem to think you are, you won't let my friend find you here."

He freed the gal from ignorance on that score. "I'm a nut, baby. A six-four, two-hundred-pound nut."

"You damn sure act like one," she shot back. She started to keep up the argument, but then she got cunning. Her smile was that sly one again. She squirmed and brought a different kind of weapon into the fight.

She fell back on her elbows, lifted one foot to the end of the bed, and the flimsy negligee rustled back over the softness of her lavish thigh. "Why do we have to spend our energy fighting," she purred lazily in that husky bedroom voice, looking up at him through half-closed eyes. Her hair, glistening and changing colors with every motion of her head, was fanned out over the chartreuse silk spread like the feathers of a peacock's tail. Tramp or not, the babe was one glamorous piece of game. "I can't tell you anything about that reporter, simply because I don't know anything about him. And pretty, since you've wrestled with me and got me feeling all unnecessary, I wish you would take me out of this strain."

"Uh-uh."

"Can't I do anything that will please you?" she said. She slow-dragged on the word 'anything.' Then she wet her full red lips with the tip of her tongue and crawled back and forth across the word. "Anything, pretty, anything."

That look she was giving him was familiar. It was supposed to make his temperature ram the thousand mark. His temperature was ramming the thousand mark, all right, but news was what he needed more than her. And this lusty bundle of sex had a lot on her mind about the murdered reporter, enough to make her willing to give all kinds of good-loving to a stranger to keep him from asking about it. But the murder raps on him and Tess and Jock made that impossible for him to do.

"Put your clothes down, baby," he told her. "You're a big girl now."

A series of expressions flashed across her face. First, one of incredulity. Then another of disbelief. Finally an expression of unmixed hatred settled on her lovely face and twisted it nastily. She slid her foot to the floor and sprang up from the bed. Her arms were tight against her sides, bent slightly at the elbows, and her small fists were clenched so hard he thought the skin over her knuckles would pop open.

"Get out, you bastard!" she panted. Her nostrils were flaring wide enough to get a pair of junior league baseball bats up them. "Get out of my apartment. And, damn it, I mean right now!"

"We got a conversation coming up."

"Go home and talk to your baby sister!"

Getting out a cigarette and a match. Tabor scratched his thumbnail across the match head. When he stuck fire to the cigarette he didn't make the mistake of looking away from Nina gal. He didn't want the babe getting any ideas about her little equalizer again. He shook out the match and went over and put his back to the dresser to discourage any gun ideas she might have.

Then he looked around the bed room. "Real nice," he remarked, nodding slowly. "Tell me. How'd you do it? Six months ago you were hustling drinks out of third-rate joints. Now you're shacking up in a penthouse, pushing a couple of new Caddies, going to the ritziest joints, and flinging twenty-dollar tips at every smiling soul in a waiter's uniform. How do you do it, baby? Tell me."

Chapter Twenty

Nina walked back to the bed and sat on the foot of it. She sat there with her arms folded tightly over her stomach and rocked back and forth a little, patting her mule-clad foot.

Smiling smoothly down at her, he pushed on. "Here's the way I've got it figured: A murdered reporter, plus your sudden exit from a seven-buck-a-week rooming house to a four-hundred-a-month penthouse, plus some other things I know, add up to one thing—blackmail."

The rocking ceased and the babe's nostrils had that fear-pinched look about them again.

The record player cut off, clicked and started up again, pouring out the same song. He said: "I don't think you'd appreciate it a bit if somebody would put out a rumor about you intending to cross the boys who bumped the newspaper guy. After you squeeze half a million out of them, of course. Even if wasting you away would get some of them burned, they'd do you in anyway. You know that."

The words gushed out of her as if someone had whammed her in her creamy belly. "I—I don't know anything, Tank." She had begun to shake like she'd just walked out of the hot broiling sun into an icy shower.

Tabor quietly dropped the name he was trying to connect with the reporter's killing. "Look what happened to Ritchie Andrews."

Nina baby went to pieces. Her face seemed to break up, to become like heated putty that was trying to run in every direction at once. She began to weave. He stepped up to the bed and caught her by her shoulders just as a set of chimes began to tinkle. He paused, cocked his head. Somebody was at Nina's door. He walked to the dresser and got the babe's little pearl-handled equalizer. He dropped the gun into his jacket pocket and started out the room to answer the door.

Nina's voice halted him.

"No!" She moved her head from side to side. "Let it

ring. I want to talk to you a-a-about the reporter." She seemed to have used all of her strength getting that last word out.

The door chimes tinkled several more times. Then suddenly the apartment was quiet except for the low moaning sax music coming from the record player and Nina Massey's strained breathing. Getting out her gun, he unloaded it, put the slugs into his pocket, and put the gun by the head of the bed. Then he sat on the bed waiting for her to get herself together.

Tess and Kate and Jock kept coming to his mind. He wondered if they were all right. They'd be doing a lot of heavy worrying about him, he thought, if he didn't show back soon.

"Why do you want to be mean to me?" Nina asked in a little girl's voice. "Why, Tank?"

"You got it a little twisted. It's just that I've got to get the answers to a lot of questions or some very good friends of mine will go to prison for some things they didn't do."

"What does the law have against them?"

"Murder," he said. "Tell me about the reporter. Everything you know."

"What do you know about Ritchie Andrews?"

"Quite a bit. I'd known him for years before he was killed. Why?"

Nina shuddered. "Ritchie was my step-brother. They murdered him."

"They?"

"Arky Calahan and his bunch." The girl searched his face carefully with troubled eyes. "You weren't sent over here to kill me, were you, Tank?"

"Calahan didn't send me here."

Nina stared up at the ceiling a while and then began to talk slowly. "I had heard on the radio about the newspaper reporter getting killed, but didn't know who'd done it until Ritchie told me. That was the night he was murdered. He called me. Told me Arky Calahan was going to kill him. I don't know how he found out about it; he didn't say. But he knew and wanted me to drive to Eighth and Wells and pick him up. Said he was scared to call his wife or go near her because he thought some of Arky's men would be in their apartment. When I got to Eighth and Wells, the patrol wagon was just taking his body away."

She paused and Tabor asked her: "Ritchie tell you who knocked off the reporter?"

Nina hesitated a moment, biting her lip, before she said quietly: "Ritchie was one of the men. He drove the follow-up car that was supposed to take out any interference. Moe and Trigger Slim were in the lead car; Slim drove and Moe did the shooting, so Ritchie told me. He wanted me to know everything in case they got him before I could pick him up, so I could tell the Feds about it."

She was silent a moment. Then, toying with a button on his shirt, she looked up at him, giving him the baby-eyed treatment.

"Maybe you think I'm a dog, for not going to the FBI men like Ritchie told me. And maybe I am. But I don't really know anything, not enough for the law to do anything with anyway. What Ritchie told me would be hearsay evidence and you know, in a courtroom, that kind doesn't go."

When Nina had finished fighting her case of accessory after the fact, Tabor asked her: "Why'd Arky have Ritchie killed? Ritchie tell you?"

"No, but I found out. One of Arky's men—a slob called Albino—told me Ritchie was spotted at the scene of the crime and that Arky knew Ritchie couldn't stand up under police pressure. So—" Nina moved her shoulders.

She didn't need to finish it. He knew what she meant.

"And the reporter?"

"Ritchie said the newspaperman had dug up enough of Arky's dirt to get him and his hoodlums life in prison. Ritchie didn't say what the evidence was though."

"Calahan the one you're putting the squeeze on?"

"Yes. But don't let anybody else know about it."

"I can't pick up yet," he said. "What I want to know is how'd you keep him from doing you in after you told him you knew his boys had done in the reporter?"

"Easy." Nina giggled. "I told him Ritchie overheard them planning to kill him and had written and signed a confession telling everything and sent it to me. I told him I'd given the confession to a friend of mine. With instructions to mail it to the Feds if I am ever missing from the city for more than two days."

"I see." He nodded. "*Did* Ritchie send you a confession?"

"No."

He looked questioningly at her, one eyebrow slightly raised. "Mean you've been conning Calahan, selling him a bluff?"

Nina giggled again. "That's all I could sell. With what Ritchie told me I convinced Arky that I knew the whole story. He had no way of knowing Ritchie hadn't sent me a signed confession. So he paid."

"How much?"

"The first payment was a tax-free hundred grand. Now I let him send me twenty-five thousand a month. Bastard that he is, I think I'm being rather nice about the whole thing, don't you?"

Tabor grinned his admiration. He was glad to meet anybody who could do it to Arky Calahan.

"Tank."

He looked at Nina. "I'm listening."

Her eyes sleepy-looking, she lay back on the bed and drew up her legs until her feet were flat on the bed, causing the sheer negligee to slide back over her smooth round thighs and settle in soft folds across her flat stomach. Huskily she said, "Are we done with business?"

He got to his feet, clamping down hard on his control. Even though the doll looked like she could work, he didn't want to play with her. A couple of days ago he would have. But not now. Not with Tess waiting for him.

"Uh-uh, doll. Just tell me where I can find Goaldie and I'll be on my way. Naturally I don't want Calahan and his hoods around while I talk to her. Can you fix that?"

For a minute he thought lovely Nina was going to deny knowing the chippie. She moved her head, getting ready to shake him off, but then, with what he thought was a flash of cunning in her eyes, she said: "Be at Arky's bar around closing time tonight. Goaldie'll be there—alone."

"Where's she now?"

Nina shrugged vaguely. "Arky's got her, I think."

Tabor nodded, lit a cigarette, then asked the lovely:

"How come you know Arky's got Goaldie and didn't know about my rumble with him?"

"She was supposed to call me today and didn't; I wanted to take her shopping with me. So I called Albino's pad. He wasn't shopping, but his girl Rose told me she thinks he took Goaldie to Arky's. If Arky's got her I'll get her for you."

That was one thing he was pretty sure of. He smoked a little and asked her: "What's between you and Goaldie?"

Nina moved her head on the bed. "Nothing. I just

knew her mother and her old man. They're doing time now. But when they were out they were all right with me so I try to be all right with their kid." She yawned prettily, stretched her long legs their full length and reached her arms up to him. "Come on." She winked and gave him a stimulating exhibition of her body action. "I feel dull," she purred. "Come put some life into me."

The willpower it took for him to shake his head had to come all the way up from his toenails. He got rid of his cigarette, swallowed a time or two to moisten his throat, then told her: "Don't try getting me wasted like you had those other four boys who got a bit too curious about your business. You would get absolutely nowhere, believe me."

"I won't, pretty," she said softly, but he knew he could believe her as much as you could believe a salesman who told you he'd forget about his commission. "Why don't you stay and let me prove I like you," she murmured throatily, and wet her ripe red lips. "I know all about love."

"Luscious one, I'll have to take your word for it this time." He sighed regretfully.

Chapter Twenty-One

From Nina Massey's hotel Tabor drove to an all-night drugstore on Fifth and Wisconsin and called the doctor's home. Waiting, he went over the thing he was planning to do. He began to sweat. One slip and tomorrow he'd be just a memory, Arky Calahan would still be top dog and Tess and Jock would still have two first-degree murder raps hanging over their heads.

Jock answered the phone. "Who is it?"

"Me, Tank. But don't tell Tess and Kate. No sense in

upsetting them any more than they already are."

"They're upstairs."

"Good. Listen. That FBI agent you told me about. Think he still wants Calahan and his mob?"

"Once those boys get to wanting somebody they keep right on wanting him until he's either proven clean or dead. You got something?"

"Maybe. Now listen good." Sweating profusely, Tabor talked for almost five minutes. He told the big guy about his visit with Nina Massey, about what he planned to do, and asked him to look out for Kate and Tess if his plan went sour. "That's it," he finished. "Think you can do it?"

"Yeah," Jock said. "I think I can, but we'll be out in the hot broiling sun without any shade, so to speak. Suppose Arky clams up? What then? You'll be right in the middle of his mob and the law, and the Feds are going to have me. Because I'll have to go back and try to keep them from grabbing you before you have a chance to try your gimmick. With both of us in the slammer that'll leave the girls wide open for anything Arky'll want to throw at 'em."

"I know it's a puny chance," he agreed, "but it's the only chance I see to get us from under Calahan's hammer. Miss this one and there may not be another. I've got to take it, as puny as it is." He looked at his watch. "It's twenty after one now. Think you can get everything set up before two? I'd like to be on the scene a few minutes before closing time."

"I'll try."

"You couldn't do any more. See you," he said and then realized he'd been talking into a dead phone. When he put the receiver on the hook he was smiling. The big guy would come through for him again, and he had a confession to write in the meantime.

Tabor cruised by Calahan's bar. The joint looked empty except for the little chippie Goaldie sitting midway down the bar and a bulky-shouldered bartender leaning over it. The guy looked like he was counting the pores on Goaldie's stomach.

When he had passed the place, he looked both ways along the street. Besides the car he was in, a half-ton panel truck in the driveway across the street from The Blue Goat was the only other vehicle in sight in the block. He drove to the corner, parked on Wells Street, got out, and ambled back toward Calahan's joint.

Somewhere in the east thunder rumbled ominously. There was the clean fresh smell of water in the air. Rain would be coming down soon, he thought, and wondered if he'd be around to see it. He liked summer rain.

He stopped in the dim-lit doorway of the pawn shop two doors from The Blue Goat and lit a cigarette. A patrol car cruised by, its motor purring softly, and Tabor felt the short hairs on the back of his neck get rigid when the driver slowed up to peer back at him. Then they went on and he began breathing again.

The block was empty now. He consulted his watch. Five to two. Then, for the eighth or ninth time since he had put it on a few minutes ago, his hand moved up to touch the artificial red carnation in the lapel of his coat. He was glad Jock was a little bigger than he was. With Jock's suit on, the small metal box strapped to the inside of his thigh had less chance of showing.

Since the patrol car had gone by, no cars had passed through the block. Everything was quiet. He took a final drag off his cigarette, flipped it toward the gutter, and walked up to The Blue Goat.

When he entered the place he saw that he had been right about the barman exploring Goaldie's anatomy.

Another inch or so and the chippie's dress would have been up around her ears. All she had on under it was pink flesh.

As Tabor walked in the bartender straightened up from over the bar and eyed him sullenly, his thickened lips clamped tight. With apparent reluctance Goaldie let her dress fall to the upper part of her pink thighs. She didn't even glance Tabor's way. Besides those two, there was nobody else in the place—that he could see.

He halted beside her stool. Her body odor and dime-store perfume had the air around her smelling loud. "Hello, Goaldie," he said.

The chippie sipped at her drink, then lowered it and began making symmetric circles on the bar with the wet bottom of her glass, ignoring him completely, as if he were not there. She acted as if she had been assured that she needn't worry about him and he was positive of this when an oily voice in back of him asked:

"Tryin' to get yourself a piece of pig meat, Tank?"

The voice belonged to Trigger Slim. Tabor turned his head slowly to look in the back bar mirror. Arky Calahan, dressed in another of his cheap mail-order suits and flanked by Trigger Slim and Monkey Face Moe, was standing a few feet inside the doorway. All of them had guns centered on his body.

Talking around the cigar butt jutting from the side of his mouth, Calahan told the girl: "Get his gun, Goaldie, and slide it up the bar. You, Tank, get your hands up. Way up."

He did as he was ordered. He had read Nina Massey right.

"And some people think you're booted," Goaldie sneered, as she snatched his gun from the holster. "You're a sucker, a hood."

Tabor looked down at her flushed face. Her eyes, bright and slitted, were laughing contemptuously at him. Sixteen though she was, the little chippie was a veteran bitch, and one with not much more life ahead of her. Dope had sucked her eyes far back into her head and underlined them with a network of tiny dark lines. Another year or two on stuff and anybody in town would be able to find her the following Decoration Day. Funny, after all the grief she'd caused him, he felt nothing for her, no anger, no hatred, not even dislike.

"Yeah, yeah, yeah," she jeered shrilly. "I said a sucker an' a hood an' I hope you don't like it."

Calahan said, "Goaldie, knock it off. You and Harry wait around in the car. Move on to the back wall, Tank, and face around."

Tabor walked around Goaldie to the rear wall and turned around. What he saw through the doorway stopped him from wondering where Arky Calahan and his boys had come from. The rear door of the half-ton panel truck in the driveway across the street was hanging open. As Calahan and Slim and Moe moved in on him, Tabor kept his face expressionless. But sweat from his scalp was trickling down the back of his neck.

Before he followed Goaldie outside, the bartender called down the room to Calahan. "Boss, want I should lock the door?"

"Just draw the blind and pull it to. We won't be long," Calahan told him, stopping a couple of paces from Tabor. "Turn off the neon."

After the bartender had gone, Trigger Slim chuckled. "I gotta go along with Goaldie, Tank. You're a sucker."

"Yeah," Tabor agreed. "Could be."

For a while longer Calahan continued to stare at him, his thick lips almost flat. Finally he asked him; "Where's Kate Lamain and Tess Andrews?"

Relief sped through Tabor's body. He breathed a little

easier. Before they killed him they wanted some information. They'd get some all right.

"They're gabbing with the D. A., I guess."

"That's a lie. Neither of those dames have been seen around the D. A.'s office."

"On the street, either, for that matter," Slim put in. "Not since you took Kate outta my place yesterday."

Moe didn't say anything, just kept his dull eyes trained on Tabor's face and his sawed-down .45 on his belly button. After giving it some thought, Calahan made him an offer.

"Tell you what, Tank. Show me where I can find Kate and Jock Adams and you and Tess Andrews got my okay to leave Milwaukee."

"Want to get us together so you can murder all of us at once, eh?"

"That's crazy talk. I'm willing to let you and Tess slide if you leave town. Do we deal?"

"Make a deal!" Tabor said. His voice was low. It trembled with all the hell he'd gone through in the past three days. He leaned forward slightly. "First you frame me with armed robbery and feeding cocaine to that little tramp Goaldie; next you had Moe and Slade torture and kill my brother and set me up to take the rap; then you had Tess Andrews raped; and tried to have Kate Lamain murdered; and you want to make a deal with me." He laughed, but it was a sound without humor.

Calahan bit down harder on his cigar butt, scowling. He made an impatient motion with his gun. "All of you begged for what you got. Those charges on you I'll get dropped. Are we doing business?"

Tabor dragged the back of his hand across his mouth. Then he nodded. "Yeah. Certainly. Just as soon as you bring my brother back to life."

Calahan's lip flattened all the way out. Trigger Slim

thumbed back the hammer of his gun. "Arky, we give it to him here?"

Calahan opened his mouth to speak but Tabor talked fast. "Wait a minute. I've changed my mind." His upraised arms felt as if they were about to come loose from his shoulders. "We can do business, Arky, only not on your terms."

"Don't stop."

"Okay, here's what I'll do if you lay off my friends and me. I'll give you all of the documented evidence I've got telling why you had that newspaper reporter killed and who you sent to do the job. That's the deal I'm giving." There was a sudden silence in the bar.

The expression on Calahan's flat face was intense. Tabor's mouth was dry. His throat was constricted. If he got over this hump maybe he'd make it. He wanted to lower his arms but he didn't dare move. He knew a movement or a sound might release the violence that flared in Calahan's eyes.

Then Calahan spoke. His voice was quiet. "Who have you been talking to, Tank?"

"One of your own men. Albino. How'd you figure I knew you were holding Kate Lamain out at Trigger Slim's place? In his confession Albino says Slim drove the car and Moe did the job on the reporter; Ritchie followed them in another car, running interference. He also tells about Ritchie holing up in his pad because somebody spotted him at the scene of the crime, and about you having Ritchie knocked off when you decided he wouldn't be able to hold out under questioning by the Illinois police. I've got all of that right here." Tabor patted his side pocket. The arm was so tired he let it stay down and lowered the other one too. Nobody told him to get them back up. "Albino's statement is only a small part of the evidence I got."

His flat eyes searching Tabor's face, Calahan told

Trigger Slim: "See what he's got in his pocket."

Slim moved up to him, taking great care not to bring his gun within Tabor's reach, and fingered the folded piece of lined writing paper out of his pocket. While Slim looked at the paper, Tabor went on lying to Calahan.

"I know you know I've talked to Nina Massey because she's the one who tipped you off about my coming here. What I bet she didn't tell you, though, is that she also gave me a signed statement telling about Ritchie calling and telling her how you intended to have him murdered and all about that newspaper reporter. Everything. He—"

Trigger Slim, the veins in his skinny neck swelling, suddenly started cursing viciously.

"What's on the paper?" Calahan asked him impatiently.

"All the details about how we knocked off that nosy newspaper guy. Every goddamn thing Tank told us! That gutless bastard Albino ratted out on us but good. Always said we shoulda rubbed out that loud-mouthed, two-bit pimp!"

Suddenly Monkey Face Moe broke his long silence. "Lemme see," he said, and held out his hand to Slim. When he got the piece of paper he glanced at it briefly and then looked up at Tabor again. "Albino write this thing?"

"Sure he did. See his name on it, don't you? I—" He broke off, staring at the paper falling from Moe's hand to the dirty barroom floor, and he knew he had flubbed out somehow.

Moe's next words told him how. "Albino can't read or write."

They had him cold.

Calahan moved forward to jam the bore of his gun into Tabor's stomach. His breath was loaded with the smell of onions.

"Give it to me straight. Who told you about the reporter?"

"I already told you," he said, thinking there was no sense in switching horses in the middle of the stream. He sucked in his breath, but Calahan's gun followed his belly, "Albino copped out. Told you that."

"Moe says Albino can't read or write. I take his word over yours." Then Calahan's eyes got droopy. He began to curse softly. "The rotten, dirty, double-dealing bitch. She's the only other person who could've blabbed all that stuff to you—that Nina Massey."

"You're wrong."

"I'll take the chance." Calahan backed away from him, his heavy lips tightening over his teeth. "Take this punk out on the lake. Then we'll pay Nina a visit." He stuffed his gun in his back pocket and turned abruptly and strode toward the door.

With Trigger Slim and Moe poking him in his kidneys with the bores of their guns, Tabor followed Calahan's boxcar figure. Sweat was streaming down his face. He tasted its saltiness on his lips. If anything was going to happen, it was supposed to happen now.

It did.

When Calahan pulled open the door he stopped so suddenly that he was off balance momentarily. Two men holding Tommy guns like they knew how to use them blocked the doorway. Behind them, out on the sidewalk, were two more men.

One of the men in front, a clean-looking young guy in a blue serge suit, told Calahan: "I'm FBI agent Prentiss. We'll take over."

For a few seconds Calahan stood as if frozen, staring up at the agent. Then he swiveled his head around to glare at Tabor. "You set this up?"

Grinning at him, Tabor nodded. Calahan's face was

as sweaty as his had been a second ago. "I did just that."

"We're clean."

"Wanna bet?"

FBI agent Prentiss nudged Calahan back with the snout of the submachine gun and the other three agents moved inside. All of them had Thompson subs.

"Drop those guns," Prentiss ordered Slim and Moe.

The hoods didn't hesitate. Staring bug-eyed and slack-jawed at the impressive display of Tommy guns, they moved over to the bar and laid down their guns with care, as if they were loaded with nitroglycerin.

After Prentiss had watched one of the other agents get Calahan's iron and go over Moe and Trigger Slim for other weapons, he looked at Tabor. "That was a long chance you took, but it paid off."

"Was the only one I had," he said. "You see the girl and the bartender out there."

The agent nodded. "Your friend Adams has them in the car."

Calahan glared at Prentiss. "You boys can't make anything stick. It's Tank's word against ours. One against three won't hold up in court. Hell, he's even wanted for three counts of murder."

Grinning, Tabor pointed out the error in his adding. "Arky, you and your boys won't be convicted on my say-so alone," he told him. "Uh-uh. Your own words are going to get all of you burned." He cupped his hand around the artificial red carnation in his lapel. "This baby is a microphone, part of a sending set that happens to be strapped to the inside of my thigh, and, everything we said was picked up by an FBI mobile central center."

Panting like a trapped animal, Calahan looked around at the sober faces of the FBI agents for confirmation of Tabor's statement.

Prentiss answered his silent question. "We have recordings of everything that has been said in here since Tabor walked in."

Chapter Twenty-Two

Three weeks later Tabor and Tess were aboard the *S. S. Evangeline* on their way to Nassau for their honeymoon. They were stretched out in deck chairs enjoying the clean smell of the mild watery breeze and watching the fiery ball of the sinking sun as it dipped slowly below the wet horizon. He and Tess had been married exactly thirty hours and he was so tickled about the whole thing that he wondered if it were a sin for one person to feel so good.

Of course a lot of his happiness was due to the way things had turned out.

Calahan and Trigger Slim and Monkey Face Moe had sung up a storm in court, so they'd get a stiff term in the jug. The State of Wisconsin has no death penalty and if they'd had to face the murder rap for the killing of the reporter in Illinois, they'd be cooked. Illinois has a death sentence.

It had been their singing, plus the chirping of Goaldie, Albino, and Nina Massey that had persuaded the jury to bring in a not-guilty verdict on Tabor and Tess and Jock on those two murder charges, which had been reduced to second degree. First degree charges wouldn't have stuck with glue.

Also, Calahan's singing had caused two high-ranking detectives, a judge, and an alderman to be awaiting trial along with him and his hoods. The other charges against Tabor had been dropped in the district attorney's office as soon as the D. A. heard those FBI tape recordings.

"Tank."

He rolled over on his side to look across the two feet of space that separated him and Tess. She smiled at him, puckering her red lips a bit. With a dress on this gal was something plus to look at. But in an outfit that revealed her glistening sun-browned thighs, as the white playsuit she wore now was doing, she looking like a delicacy.

"Tank, you know we only have a month to honeymoon before we have to go back for Arky's trial."

"What's on your beautiful mind, hon?"

"As if you didn't know." Grinning back at him, Tess stood up. She stood there, looking down impishly at him, with her hands on her lovely hips. "Well, come on, Tank. We can't make up for lost time out here in front of all these people." Then she went laughingly toward their cabin.

That gal sure could make the most sensible talk, Tabor thought. He scrambled to his feet and trotted after her, grinning lecherously.

THE END

GLOSSARY OF UNDERWORLD LINGO

booster – a dope addict
booted – special person; notable
bread – money
cannon – a gunman; gun
cheese-eater – a squealer
cooling it – hiding out
crib – house
crumb crushers – teeth
Decoration Day – Memorial Day (a US holiday)
dukes – fists
Dutch lunch – an individual serving of assorted sliced cold meats and cheeses
fly-cat – a weird person
fly-guy – A very cool person or someone regarded as appealing in a sociable way; hip.
gandy dancer – itinerant laborer
gangway – alley, hall
geets – money
greenies – dollars
hooker – prostitute
jasper – homosexual (woman)
Jodie – a guy; man
juice – liquor
knowledge knot – head
mackman – pimp
penitentiary pork – jail bait
queenie – homosexual (man)
rancho – house
running-buddy – friend
short – a car (automobile); originally: street car
simoleons – dollars
slammer – jail
slides – pockets
swoop – leave
torch – cigarette lighter
tyro – novice
wig, a wig – terrific, the greatest

William Hector Duhart was born in Florida on January 30, 1921. He had the distinction of being only one of two Black authors to attend the Handy Writers Colony, opened in 1950 by Lowney and Harry Handy and novelist James Jones in Marshall, Illinois, which supported numerous young writers in the 1950s and early 60s. Duhart worked at the Colony on *The Deadly Pay-Off*—begun in Wisconsin State Prison where he served time for assault and armed robbery—which was published by Gold Medal Books in 1958. He published one other novel and a handful of short stories, and copyrighted at least six screenplays that were never produced. Duhart died at age 81 in Illinois on January 14, 2003.

Black Gat Books is a new line of mass market paperbacks introduced in 2015 by Stark House Press. New titles appear every other month, featuring the best in crime fiction reprints. Each book is size to 4.25" x 7", just like they used to be. Collect them all.

Harry Whittington · A Haven for the Damned #1 ·

Charlie Stella · Eddie's World #2

Leigh Brackett · Stranger at Home #3

John Flagg · The Persian Cat #4

Malcolm Braly · Felony Tank #6

Vin Packer 8 The Girl on the Best Seller List #7

Orrie Hitt · She Got What She Wanted #8

Helen Nielsen · The Woman on the Roof #9

Lou Cameron · Angel's Flight #10

Gary Lovisi · The Affair of Lady Westcott's Lost Ruby / The Case of the Unseen Assassin #11

Arnold Hano · The Last Notch #12

Clifton Adams · Never Say No to a Killer #13

Ed Lacy · The Men From the Boys #14

Henry Kane · Frenzy of Evil #15

William Ard · You'll Get Yours #16

Bert & Dolores Hitchens · End of the Line #17

Noël Calef · Frantic #18

Ovid Demaris · The Hoods Take Over #19

Fredric Brown · Madball #20

Louis Malley Stool Pigeon #21

Frank Kane · The Living End #22

Ferguson Findley · My Old Man's Badge #23

Paul Connolly · Tears are for Angels #24

E. P. Fenwick · Two Names for Death #25

Lorenz Heller · Dead Wrong #26

Robert Martin · Little Sister #27

Calvin Clements · Satan Takes the Helm #28

Jack Karney · Cut Me In #29

George Benet · The Hoodlums #30

Jonathan Craig · So Young, So Wicked #31

Edna Sherry · Tears for Jessie Hewitt #32

William O'Farrell · Repeat Performance #33

Marvin Albert · The Girl With No Place to Hide #34

Edward S. Aarons · Gang Rumble #35

William Fuller · Back Country #36

Robert Silverberg · The Killer #37

William R. Cox · Make My Coffin Strong #38

A. S. Fleischman · Blood Alley #39

Harold R. Daniels · The Girl in 304 #40

Stark House Press
1315 H Street, Eureka, CA 95501 (707) 498-3135
griffinskye3@sbcglobal.net www.starkhousepress.com
Available from your local bookstore or direct from the publisher

www.ingramcontent.com/pod-product-compliance
Lightning Source LLC
LaVergne TN
LVHW021817060526
838201LV00058B/3418